"About that kiss..."

Jodie began. "I thought you were your brother, so I thought a kiss would be an icebreaker."

"You don't want me to tell my brother, is that it?" Donovan asked.

"That isn't 'it' at all. I just didn't want you thinking I went around kissing strange men like that."

"I may be frustrated some of the time, but I'm not strange."

Irritation tensed her jaw. "You know perfectly well what I meant."

His golden-brown eyes laughed at her. "Your secret is safe with me."

"Would you stop...it's *not* a secret."

"You worry too much. It's no big deal."

It's no big deal. Jodie drew a deep, calming breath into her lungs. It had *seemed* simple, coming to Alaska. She could give her children a father, build a new life in the place she'd loved as a child.

Simple.

Until she'd mistakenly kissed her fiancé's brother....

Dear Reader,

Looking for sensational summer reads? All year we've been celebrating Silhouette's 20th Anniversary with special titles, and this month's selections are just the warm, romantic tales you've been seeking!

Bestselling author Stella Bagwell continues the newest Romance promotion, AN OLDER MAN. *Falling for Grace* hadn't been his intention, particularly when his younger, *pregnant* neighbor was carrying his nephew's baby! Judy Christenberry's THE CIRCLE K SISTERS miniseries comes back to Romance this month, when sister Melissa enlists the temporary services of *The Borrowed Groom*. Moyra Tarling's *Denim & Diamond* pairs a rough-hewn single dad with the expectant woman he'd once desired beyond reason...but let get away.

Valerie Parv unveils her romantic royalty series THE CARRAMER CROWN. When a woman literally washes ashore at the feet of the prince, she becomes companion to *The Monarch's Son*...but will she ever become the monarch's wife? Julianna Morris's BRIDAL FEVER! persists when *Jodie's Mail-Order Man* discovers his heart's desire: the *brother* of her mail-order groom! And Martha Shields's *Lassoed!* is the perfect Opposites Attract story this summer. The sparks between a rough-and-tumble rodeo champ and the refined beauty sent to photograph him jump off every page!

In future months, look for STORKVILLE, USA, our newest continuity series. And don't miss the charming miniseries THE CHANDLERS REQUEST... from *New York Times* bestselling author Kasey Michaels.

Happy reading!

Mary-Theresa Hussey

Mary-Theresa Hussey
Senior Editor

Please address questions and book requests to:
Silhouette Reader Service
U.S.: 3010 Walden Ave., P.O. Box 1325, Buffalo, NY 14269
Canadian: P.O. Box 609, Fort Erie, Ont. L2A 5X3

Jodie's
Mail-Order Man

JULIANNA MORRIS

Published by Silhouette Books
America's Publisher of Contemporary Romance

With much appreciation to Mandy and the Fairbanks Convention & Visitors Bureau.

SILHOUETTE BOOKS

ISBN 0-373-19460-9

JODIE'S MAIL-ORDER MAN

Copyright © 2000 by Martha Ann Ford

This edition published by arrangement with Harlequin Books S.A.

Visit Silhouette at www.eHarlequin.com

Printed in U.S.A.

Books by Julianna Morris

Silhouette Romance

Baby Talk #1097
Family of Three #1178
Daddy Woke Up Married #1252
Dr. Dad #1278
The Marriage Stampede #1375
*Callie, Get Your Groom #1436
*Hannah Gets a Husband #1448
*Jodie's Mail-Order Man #1460

*Bridal Fever!

JULIANNA MORRIS

has an offbeat sense of humor, which frequently gets her into trouble. She is often accused of being curious about everything...her interests ranging from oceanography and photography to traveling, antiquing, walking on the beach and reading science fiction. Choosing a college major was extremely difficult, but after many changes she earned a bachelor's degree in environmental science.

Julianna's writing is supervised by a cat named Gandalf, who sits on the computer monitor and criticizes each keystroke. Ultimately, she would like a home overlooking the ocean, where she can write to her heart's content—and Gandalf's malcontent. She'd like to share that home with her own romantic hero, someone with a warm, sexy smile, lots of patience and an offbeat sense of humor to match her own. Oh, yes...and he has to like cats.

Chapter One

"You aren't going to marry him, not *really*... Are you, Mom?"

Jodie pulled two suitcases down from the luggage rack, then looked at her eight-year-old son. "This is just a getting-acquainted trip, Tadd. I told you that."

"*Puleeze,* the guy's an accountant." He slouched deeper in his airplane seat. Tadd said *accountant* the way some people said ax murderer, and Jodie sighed.

"You were the one who said I should get married again," she reminded him. "I'm sure you'll like Mr. Masters if you give him a chance. He's a friend of your uncle David. They met when David was stationed here in Alaska."

"I wanted you to marry someone like Dad," Tadd mumbled, his face rebellious. "Not an accountant."

Jodie's heart twinged. She did *not* want to marry someone like her first husband. Air force pilot Mark

Richards had been the most exciting, wonderful thing in her life—until he died in a routine training mission because he was going too fast and taking too many chances.

No, give her someone quiet and settled like a tax accountant. Forget romance; this time she wanted a sensible marriage based on common interests and goals. She didn't need the heartache.

Jodie unbuckled her daughter's seat belt. Penny looked up, a sunny smile on her little face. "New daddy, Mama?"

The tight ache in Jodie's chest eased. Penny embraced life with a joyful exuberance. She didn't worry or fuss or think about what might have been. And unlike her brother, she was thrilled about the prospect of getting a new father.

"Maybe, sweetheart."

"Bye, Penny," said an elderly couple as they edged past them in the airplane aisle. They weren't the first to say goodbye—half their fellow passengers had stopped to say something before disembarking.

Jodie looked at her daughter and shook her head, laughing. Penny collected new friends the way some people collected baseball cards.

"Come on, munchkin. Let's get out of here. Go with your brother."

Tadd took his sister's hand, leading the two-year-old down the aisle and out of the plane. As they stepped into the terminal, Jodie looked around, searching for the man whose picture she'd studied a hundred times.

There he is.

At least she thought it was him. The man standing a few yards away seemed different—more defined than his photograph, more mature and sensual than she'd imagined he would be. Her heart beat faster.

Just nerves, she rationalized. She'd never been a mail-order bride before. Even now she could hardly believe she was doing anything so unconventional. Anyway, she *should* feel attracted to her future husband, even if she wasn't in love with him. There was nothing wrong with warmth and a pleasant tingle, as long as they were mixed with mutual respect. Right?

Gritting her teeth, Jodie put a brake on her thoughts. She was mentally babbling, something that happened when she got nervous.

The man straightened and locked gazes with her for a long minute. He seemed to be waiting for something and Jodie wondered if he was feeling the same quick rush of awareness.

"That's him," Tadd muttered. "The accountant."

Penny dropped her brother's hand. "Daddy," she shrieked happily. She ran full tilt at the stranger and threw her arms around his leg.

A startled expression crossed his face. "Well...hello, there." He disengaged Penny's grip on his thigh and lifted her in his arms. She patted his cheek and gave him a noisy kiss.

Jodie smiled. Maybe her daughter had the right idea. Rather than standing around waiting for an awkward introduction, she should just give him a kiss and see what happened.

Putting the suitcases on the ground, Jodie stepped closer. A long time ago she'd been just as impulsive as Penny, just as enthusiastic about life. She drew on those memories now, to give her courage.

"Hi," she murmured. Warm, golden brown eyes looked at her, equal amounts of surprise and question in their depths. "I'm glad to finally meet you."

Before she could think better of it, Jodie slid her hand behind the back of his head and tugged. After a split second of hesitation, his firm lips moved over hers. There was a faint flavor of mint and coffee in the kiss and she instinctively drew a breath.

It was good, almost too good. The shiver that went to her tummy had nothing to do with fear. She'd dated a few times in the past year, but none of those men had made her feel a tenth this much response. Maybe it was a good omen.

Or maybe she should be scared out of her socks. A second later he lifted his head and stared into her face. "I—uh." He cleared his throat. "I'm afraid I'm not who you think."

She'd kissed a perfect stranger?

Heat burned Jodie's cheeks and she stepped back quickly. "I'm terribly sorry. You look just like…that is, I was expecting… Never mind. Come here, munchkin," she said, holding her arms out to Penny. Unfortunately her daughter was clinging to the man's neck like a limpet.

"Don't apologize. I always enjoy kissing a beautiful woman, and I got lucky today with two of them," he murmured, turning his head to give Penny a light kiss on her cheek.

"Oh." The compliment flustered Jodie. "That's nice, but we're supposed to be meeting someone. Let go of him, Penny."

"Daddy," Penny insisted.

"No, this isn't Daddy…er, Cole. Remember, we—we're just here to visit," she stuttered, nonplussed with both embarrassment and confusion. This whole thing had to sound insane to a stranger, and she wasn't too sure it didn't sound insane to her as well.

"No, my *daddy*." Ninety-nine percent of the time Penny was sweetly good-natured, but in the remaining one percent she was pure stubbornness.

"It's complicated," she said to the man, feeling she should explain why her daughter thought a stranger was her daddy.

"It usually is." Donovan looked at his brother's bride-to-be and swore silently. How could Cole put him in a position like this? Okay, so Cole had gotten a last-minute chance to join a climb on Mount McKinley. Surely the arrival of his prospective wife was a little more important.

As for the youngsters? As usual, Cole had left out a few details—like the fact Jodie Richards would be arriving with a couple of kids.

Donovan surveyed Jodie again, fighting an edgy, masculine awareness. She was slim and not too tall, with the lithe, supple grace of a cat. A green silk blouse and skirt outlined her feminine curves to perfection. For all her cool elegance, he could sense the fire burning beneath her polished surface—a fire he shouldn't have any interest in exploring. If only she hadn't kissed him. Then he wouldn't feel so…uncomfortable.

Shocked at the direction of his thoughts, Donovan cleared his throat. "Actually, I'm Cole's brother, Donovan Masters," he explained belatedly. "Pleased to meet you."

Her eyes blinked. "I thought Cole would be here."

"Yeah, well, it's a long story. I'll explain on the way."

"On the way? Where are we going?"

Doubt had replaced the embarrassed flush in her face, and Donovan sighed. Cole owed him big-time for this favor. Of course, only Cole would write to a woman he'd never met, then propose marriage after a few letters.

"Uh...let's get a cup of coffee," Donovan murmured. "I'll explain everything." He glanced at the child in his arms and the solemn boy at Jodie's elbow. "You guys feel like a milk shake?"

The little girl nodded emphatically. She was a mirror image of her mother, from the cat-green eyes to the gold silk of her hair.

"Obviously you've already met Penny," Jodie said quickly. She urged the dark-haired boy forward. "And this is my son, Tadd."

"Hello, Tadd." Donovan set Penny on the floor so he could shake hands with the reluctant boy. They were nice-looking kids, though undoubtedly Tadd took after his father. There was nothing in his brown eyes and olive skin that resembled the feminine side of the family.

"Are you an accountant, *too,* Mr. Masters?"

Donovan's eyebrows shot upward at the boy's hostile tone.

"That's enough," Jodie ordered quickly. Donovan Masters would think her son was a rude little monster, and it wasn't true. As a rule, Tadd was very well behaved; his grandfather made certain of that. She unconsciously winced at the thought of her father. General Thaddeus McBride was a career air force officer who treated his family with the same rigid discipline he drilled into his flight crews.

"Actually, I'm a pilot," Donovan murmured.

Tadd's face brightened. "In the air force?"

"No, I have an air-transit business here in Alaska."

"Wow. Did you hear that, Mom? He's a pilot, just like Dad."

Tension coiled tighter in Jodie's stomach and she gave Tadd a warning glance. "I heard him the first time."

In all the letters she and Cole had exchanged, he'd never mentioned that his thirty-six-year-old brother was a pilot. His descriptions had included phrases such as *fun-loving, laid-back,* and *doesn't take anything seriously.* But not *pilot.*

Jodie swallowed. She didn't need her son getting any smart ideas about playing matchmaker. She'd come up to meet *Cole* Masters, not his brother. Which meant she could just forget about that kiss, and Tadd could forget about her marrying a pilot "just like Dad."

"I think coffee would be a good idea, Mr. Masters. Is anything wrong with Cole?"

An odd expression crossed Donovan's face. "No, but it'll take some explaining. At any rate, please call me Donovan." He winked at Tadd. "The same goes for you."

"All right, Donovan." Tadd had the rapt face of a first-year cadet at the academy, listening to one of his favorite instructors.

Academy.

Jodie rolled her eyes. She'd grown up all over the world as an air force brat, and then she'd married

an air force officer. Heck, she was so saturated with
the air force, she couldn't think in any other way.
That was one of the reasons she wanted to marry
someone not connected with the armed services. Her
children needed to know there was a different world
out there, with different possibilities.

"There's a café down this way," Donovan murmured. He took her suitcases.

"Fine." Holding Penny's hand, Jodie followed
him down the airport concourse. It was larger than
she'd expected for the size of Fairbanks, though she
knew the town was a transportation center for the
interior of the state.

A faint thrill of excitement crept through her, despite the unexpected turn of events. Her father had
been stationed in Alaska when she was a child, right
before her mother had died. She'd loved it—even
the cold and wild storms of winter. It was a far cry
from the heat and humidity of Florida where they'd
been living for the past couple of years. There was
a part of her that had always known she'd come
back to Alaska.

"Have a seat, and I'll get the coffee and treats,"
Donovan said when they reached the coffee shop.
He put the luggage next to a table, then pulled a
chair out for Jodie. "That is…if it's all right for the
kids to have milk shakes?" he asked. "We could
get sandwiches or something."

"Milk shakes are fine," Jodie said as she settled
Penny into a chair of her own. "We ate on the
plane."

"Great. What flavor do you want, Tadd?"

"Strawberry. Penny likes it, too, but she can't

have any 'cause it makes her itch, so she has to have chocolate,'' Tadd answered.

"Is that so, Penny?"

Penny sighed with a comically adult expression. "No taw'berries."

He grinned. It was hard not to smile at Penny; she was a living ray of sunshine. A child like that could bring laughter into the darkest Alaska winter, yet it still boggled his mind that Cole was considering marriage at all, much less to a woman with two kids.

The thought nagged at Donovan as he waited in line at the cash register. The Masters family didn't have a great track record with marriage, though his mom seemed happy enough with her second husband.

Did Cole know about the children?

Perhaps Jodie had failed to mention them in her letters. Donovan glanced at the young woman across the restaurant, then shook his head. She seemed pretty direct.

Hell, *direct* was an understatement. For all its innocent brevity, that kiss had sent his temperature up ten degrees. It was hard to imagine her concealing anything.

"Here you go," he said a minute later, putting a tray down on the table. "One chocolate shake, and one strawberry. And two cups of coffee."

Tadd's eyes gleamed as he began drinking the concoction with a deliberate speed. "Grandfather doesn't like us to have ice cream in the middle of the day," he said between sips. "We can have it after dinner, but he gets upset when Mom gives us some early. Then they have a big fight."

Hmmm.

The Richardses were getting more and more interesting. Donovan handed Jodie her cup and sat
back with his own, watching her. A hundred questions begged for answers, such as: What had happened to her first husband? Were they divorced?
And why would a woman with Jodie Richards's face
and body need a mail-order marriage? One thing
was sure—she didn't look old enough to have an
eight-year-old son, but Cole had said she was in her
late twenties.

"Sounds like you and your father have some dis-
agreements over raising children," he murmured.

Jodie took a sip of the steaming coffee. She
shifted uncomfortably under Donovan's curious
gaze and shrugged. "Father can be rather strict. He
believes in three square meals a day and a very limited amount of indulgence."

"My grandfather is a two-star general," Tadd
contributed, his expression a peculiar mix of pride
and ambivalence. "We live with him."

"Look," Jodie said, setting her cup down, "I'd
like to know what's going on with Cole. He said
he'd meet us."

"Yeah." It was Donovan's turn to look uncomfortable. "He tried to call a couple of days ago, but
he couldn't reach you."

Her eyes narrowed. This didn't sound good. "I
decided to take an earlier flight and spend some time
with a friend in Denver. So, where is Cole?"

Donovan tapped his fingers on the table. "Well,
right about now he's in the preliminary stages of
climbing the West Buttress of Mount McKinley."

Jodie stared. She didn't know a great deal about
mountain climbers, but she knew they risked their

lives for the sake of climbing a chunk of rock. *A rock.* They couldn't enjoy looking at the mountain from a safe distance, they had to see it close up, coupled with risk and danger and adrenaline. She understood all about adrenaline junkies. She'd married one of them.

"So," she said carefully, trying to keep a grip on her temper, "Cole is an avid mountain climber."

Donovan nodded. "One of the best."

"That's pretty great, Mom," Tadd exclaimed. He'd finished his own milk shake and was polishing off his sister's. "Maybe he won't be so bad after all."

She spun her head around, her patience strained to the limit. "Not now, Tadd. Go look after your sister." Penny had climbed down and was exploring a rack of brightly colored postcards.

Tadd opened his mouth to protest, but a single look from his mother silenced him. Jodie was a softer touch than his grandfather, but when she laid down the law, that was that.

She waited until her son was out of immediate earshot. "Cole never said anything about being a climber."

Donovan whistled silently at the angry sparks in Jodie's eyes. He was right—there was a lot of fire inside Jodie Richards.

He cleared his throat, uncertain whether she was angry about Cole not telling of his favorite hobby, or that he'd taken off on a climb when he was supposed to be meeting her. Or maybe she was angry about both.

"Jodie, he hasn't changed his mind about the marriage, if that's what you're thinking."

"That's big of him."

Donovan leaned forward. "You have every right to be upset, but try to understand. Cole has wanted to climb McKinley ever since he was a kid. And he didn't plan for this to happen—he signed up as an alternate on the team before you talked about getting married."

Jodie took a deep breath. She understood about lifelong dreams, but it seemed as if every dire prediction her father had uttered about her trip to Alaska was coming true. That was the worst part, wondering how many times she'd have to hear "I told you so." He meant well, but he couldn't see that a family needed more than rules and hop-to commands.

"How long is this climb supposed to take?"

Donovan hesitated. "About three weeks."

Her fingers curled into her palm. "Then Cole will get back only a few days before we're supposed to leave."

"If the climb goes well, he'll be back even earlier." Donovan didn't say what would happen if the climb *didn't* go well. McKinley wasn't as dangerous as climbing a mountain like Everest, but it wasn't safe, either. "Cole said if you got married, he figured this would be his last chance to climb McKinley. I think he's planning to give up climbing if things work out...between you."

She was silent for a full minute, obviously weighing what she'd heard and making decisions. He couldn't blame her. She had her children to think about.

"Fine. We'll fly home, then come back later in the summer when he's ready."

"You can't do that." The sharpness in his voice surprised Donovan, but he didn't stop to examine the reasons. "That is, you won't be able to get a flight out. Not easily. Cruise ships bring passengers up to Alaska, then they fly home after touring the state. Outbound flights are booked for weeks ahead during the summer."

She didn't say anything and he wondered if she was still angry, or merely thinking.

"You also came to see if you like Alaska and the family," he said, using all his persuasive powers. "My mom and stepfather said you can stay with them as long as you want."

"We planned to stay in a hotel. Anyway, I lived here when I was a kid, so I know what it's like. I've always loved Alaska. I hated it when my father was transferred to Hawaii."

The last piece of information surprised him. Jodie seemed like a butterfly, soft and golden and just as delicate. He didn't know anything about that kind of woman. Didn't she belong in the sun? Exotic butterflies should live on tropical islands with warm, scented breezes.

Both amused and annoyed at the direction his mind had taken, Donovan gulped the last of his coffee. It was going to be harder than he'd thought to remember Jodie belonged to his brother. He should just drop her at his mother's house, then head south again.

"Mom has plenty of room and she'll be disappointed if you don't stay," he murmured. "You want to get acquainted with her, don't you?"

"Of course. But..." Jodie shrugged diffidently.

"It's awkward. Without Cole here, it doesn't seem right to impose, especially with Tadd and Penny."

"Believe me, it's no imposition. The only thing Mom loves more than company is children." The wry, amused tone in Donovan's voice made Jodie smile. Family was important and she wanted to be sure she got along with her proposed new in-laws.

Sudden warmth flushed her body as the memory of kissing Donovan crowded her mind. Oh...she got along with Donovan, all right, but it wasn't the kind of "all right" that was appropriate between in-laws. And just as suddenly, Jodie realized it was a good thing Donovan hadn't turned out to be Cole. She wanted to feel a moderate attraction for her husband, not a soul-burning passion. If a single kiss made her so unsettled, then marrying a man like Donovan would be too much of a risk.

"Jodie?" His hand covered her fingers and she jumped. "What do you say? A few weeks with my mother would be a great vacation. She's a good cook and you can see all the tourist spots around Fairbanks."

Her mouth dry, Jodie stared at the large male hand clasping hers. The cautious side of her said no, but the impulsive side said *yes*. She'd taken a lot of chances in her life; why not try one more time?

"I guess we could stay," she said slowly. "For a few days at least."

"Great." He stood and collected the suitcases from beside the table. "Let's go."

Chapter Two

Donovan frowned as he looked at Jodie's two suit-cases. "This doesn't look like enough for a month, not for the three of you."

"There's a larger bag I checked through," she said. "I hope it got here safely. We had to change planes a couple of times."

"Okay, we'll go to the baggage claim area first."

She called the children, lifting Penny into her arms so they could walk faster. Donovan wondered how she'd managed at each of the airports, handling both luggage and children by herself, then stopped wondering when he thought about the determined tilt to her chin.

It was too early to tell, but Jodie might be exactly what his brother needed.

Just what he needed?

Donovan mentally smacked his forehead. Cole didn't need to get married, he needed his head examined. Marrying a woman like Jodie Richards might be appealing for the obvious reasons, but Cole had never seen her outside of a photograph. No matter how gorgeous she looked in that photo, it couldn't be enough to make his brother's hormones scream "marriage."

"You got awfully quiet all of a sudden," Jodie murmured, breaking his train of thought.

He cast a glance at her, noting the healthy pink color brought to her face by the exertion of walking and carrying Penny. Maybe he was silently arguing the merits of Cole's proposed marriage because he was attracted to Jodie himself, but couldn't make any moves on her. Only a heel would flirt with his brother's fiancée.

"I was just trying to guess how you and Cole got hooked up together," Donovan answered, more or less honestly. "He mentioned you lived in Florida, but he didn't have time to explain much else."

A small frown creased Jodie's forehead, though he didn't know if she was just thinking, or annoyed again. "My brother was stationed at Eielson Air Force Base a few years ago, and they got to be friends. As the story goes, David told Cole about me and suggested we start writing to each other."

"Hmm." Donovan suspected there was a lot more to the "story" than Jodie was saying. "Sounds simple enough."

Jodie wrinkled her nose. "Not really. David is a lot like my father—which means he thinks he has the right to arrange everyone's lives. At the beginning I wasn't going to write back, but the first letter sounded interesting, so I..." She shrugged. "The McBride men can't always be wrong, even if they do have the tact of stampeding buffalo."

Donovan swallowed a laugh. He'd gotten an ab-
surd image of Jodie holding a toreador's cape as she
fended off the men in her life. "How many 'Mc-
Bride men' are there?"

"Five. Four brothers, one father."

"All air force?"

"Except for Robert. He's the black sheep in the
family—he enlisted in the navy."

"I see." Donovan didn't ask how Jodie fit into
the picture, black sheep or otherwise. It was obvious
that her family caused her a great deal of amused
exasperation.

"You can imagine how well my father accepted
the news," she added, giving him a droll smile.
"'Third-generation air force and *he* wants to wear
white sailor pants,'" she mimicked.

"I guess the rivalry between the different armed
services is just as intense as I've heard." Donovan
steered the small group downstairs.

Jodie shrugged. "At least it is for anyone who
serves under my father's command."

"Including his family?"

"*Especially* his family," she corrected. "It's
worse than being born into a dynasty. At least a
dynasty doesn't operate under military rules of en-
gagement."

Everything she said raised more questions for
Donovan, questions he didn't feel it was his place
to ask. "Here we are," he said as they approached
the baggage claim area.

To his surprise, Jodie's third suitcase wasn't much
bigger than the two she'd carried onto the plane.
From his experience with flying tourists around
Alaska, he'd gotten the notion that women always

packed too much. Apparently she wasn't guilty of that problem.

In the parking lot they belted Tadd and Penny into the back seat of the Jeep Grand Cherokee, which he'd borrowed from the local branch office of Triple M Transit. It was convenient being one-third owner of a business that provided service over most of Alaska. Whenever he visited from his home on the Kenai Peninsula, he was able to have his own ground transportation in Fairbanks.

He'd reached to open the passenger door when Jodie shifted her feet uncomfortably. "Uh, Donovan?"

His hand dropped. "Yes?" he asked cautiously.

"About what happened at the terminal...?"

"Yes?"

"I was just trying to be spontaneous. And I thought you were Cole, so I thought a kiss would be an icebreaker." Jodie stopped, deciding her explanation was just making matters worse.

"You don't want me to tell Cole, is that it?"

She gave him an annoyed look. "That isn't 'it' at all. I just didn't want you thinking I went around like that, kissing strange men."

"Boy, that hurts."

He sounded serious and she frowned. "What hurts?"

"I may be frustrated some of the time, but I'm not strange."

Irritation tensed her jaw. "You know perfectly well what I meant."

His golden-brown eyes laughed at her. "Your secret is safe with me."

Jodie's fingers tightened on the strap of her purse.

It wouldn't be civilized to hit him over the head with it, but she was tempted. "Would you stop... It's *not* a secret."

"You worry too much. It's no big deal. And I'm to blame—I should have said something when Penny ran up calling me 'Daddy.'" He opened the door and bowed, sweeping his arm down and around in a grandiose gesture. "I bet my mother is planning a great dinner to welcome you to Alaska, so we'd better head out."

Still glaring, Jodie hiked her slim-cut skirt up a couple of inches and climbed into the high seat of the vehicle. She should have worn slacks for the flight, but feminine vanity had won out over common sense.

It's no big deal.

In all honesty, she wasn't so upset about the teasing, it was the way he'd brushed off their kiss. Her lips still tingled from the brief contact with Donovan's mouth, but *he* said it wasn't a big deal.

Jodie drew a deep, calming breath into her lungs. She needed to get a grip. Women invested too much meaning into things like kisses. Men were better off without the kind of feminine second-guessing she went through.

Like now.

She twisted in the bucket seat of the vehicle, wishing life was a little simpler. It had *seemed* simple, coming to Alaska. She could get her children away from the stifling life on an air force base, give them a father and build a new life in a place she'd loved as a child.

Simple.

Until she'd mistakenly kissed her fiancé's brother

and gotten more confused than she'd felt in a long time.

Jodie looked around with restless energy. Donovan stood just outside the driver's door, talking on a cell phone. She surreptitiously studied him, trying to understand the reasons he'd affected her so strongly. Anticipation? Perhaps that was the answer. For weeks she'd anticipated meeting Cole, hoping they'd like each other in person as much as they'd liked each other in their letters. The kiss was just a culmination of all that expectation and hopeful thinking.

Donovan punched a button, then dialed another number into the phone. He said a few words, waited, then said something else, his mouth tight with apparent irritation. After a long moment he nodded and opened the door.

"It's Cole. He wanted me to call once you got here," he said, handing over the phone.

Jodie swallowed and took the cell phone. Ah, the miracles of modern life. A man could take off for a climb on Mount McKinley and still apologize to the woman he'd promised to meet.

"Hello?" she murmured into the receiver.

"God, Jodie, I'm so sorry," Cole exclaimed, his voice eerily similar to his brother's. "I didn't mean for this to happen, I swear. But they would have been forced to cancel the expedition if I didn't go."

She bit her tongue, *literally*, not wanting to say something she'd regret.

"You there, Jodie?"

"Yes. I understand this was the opportunity of a lifetime," she murmured, congratulating herself on her steady tone. "I'm glad you were able to join the climb."

"That's great of you. I've go—"

Static crackled the line and she waited, wondering what else needed to be said. "Cole?"

"Sorry. This damn phone doesn't get good reception up here, and it'll be worse the higher up we go. I can't talk long, but how did the kids take the trip? It's a long way from Florida."

"They're fine. We stopped over in Denver for a couple of days."

"That's why I couldn't reach you. Well…" His voice trailed and she could hear the sound of impatient voices in the background.

"You'd better go. We'll talk when you get back," Jodie said.

"Okay." Another crackle of static followed, then silence.

She handed the phone to Donovan, who slipped it into his shirt pocket. "Did Cole straighten everything out?"

"What's to straighten out?" she asked evenly.

"You know what I mean."

Yeah, she knew. Donovan might be easygoing and laid-back the way Cole had described, but nothing seemed to escape his notice. Donovan realized she was upset that Cole had left, and that she was upset because she ought to understand his dream of climbing Mount McKinley. And she *did* understand, except now she had to question all over again whether Cole was the right man for her to marry. Men who craved dangerous challenges didn't make ideal husbands.

"I think this is something between Cole and me,"

she said firmly. It didn't do any good to avoid Donovan's knowing gaze, so she met it squarely.

"Fine." Donovan started the engine and drove out of the lot.

Jodie glanced into the rear seat. Tadd and Penny were gazing around, curiosity in their eyes. Despite the turmoil in her thoughts, Jodie smiled at the way Tadd held his sister's hand in a protective grasp.

It had always been that way. Since the moment Penny was born, her brother had assumed the role of protector. Though hardly old enough to understand, he'd realized she was small and defenseless. For an instant her smile wavered. She'd been pregnant with Penny and had almost lost her in those terrible months after Mark died.

"Hey. It's not so terrible," Donovan murmured, watching her face. "I'm sure Tadd will decide that a mountain climber is almost as good as a pilot."

Jodie stiffened. She knew Donovan was just teasing her again. He didn't know her husband had been killed in a plane, so he couldn't understand how she felt. How could he? He was a pilot, just like Mark. And if Mark had survived that damned crash, he would have climbed aboard another jet as soon as he was able.

"Jodie?" Donovan's teasing smile faded into concern. "I didn't mean to say anything to upset you. Honest, you can't take me seriously. I joke around too much."

"Don't be silly. I'm sorry Tadd was rude," she said quietly, still keeping one eye on the back seat. Neither Penny or Tadd seemed aware of their conversation, but as the old saying went, little pitchers had big ears.

"At least Cole will always know where he stands."

"That's one way of putting it."

Donovan chuckled at Jodie's droll tone, though he sensed a forced quality in her voice. Something had brought a shadow to her catlike eyes.

With an effort he focused his attention on the road ahead. If Cole hadn't gone on that climb, then *he'd* be here, worrying about Jodie's eyes and the things that made her sad. Instead, it was big brother Donovan, always safe to call in an emergency. And it might have been safe if Jodie hadn't mistaken him for Cole and given him a kiss that nearly knocked his shoes off.

A frown creased the space between his eyes. As kisses went, that one was utterly chaste. But it had made him see her first as a woman, instead of as a potential sister-in-law.

"Do your parents live far from here?" Jodie asked a few minutes later. They'd passed the city limits and were getting into a less-populated area.

Donovan flashed her a reassuring smile. "It's just a few miles. I don't really think of Shamus as my father. I'd already moved out and was working on the Alaska pipeline when Mom remarried."

"That's too bad."

"But Cole is closer to Shamus. He was sixteen at the time, so it's more like a father-son relationship between them."

After another fifteen minutes Donovan turned down a neatly laid driveway of crushed rock. They wound through the trees for a quarter of a mile, then pulled up next to a massive log house halfway down the hill.

"It's beautiful," Jodie breathed, staring at the structure and surroundings with obvious pleasure.

"Not too bad." He went to help her out, carefully ignoring the way her skirt rode up her legs. Earlier he'd caught a glimpse of Jodie's smooth, tanned thighs and his temperature had gone up another few degrees, no doubt explaining his foul temper when he'd called Cole.

Donovan winced, thinking of the brief, biting comments he'd passed on to his little brother. He should have kept his mouth shut. The last thing Cole needed on a dangerous climb was something to break his concentration.

"Welcome to Alaska," cried a voice. Donovan looked up in time to see his mother pull Jodie into a hug. "I'm so happy to meet you."

"We're happy to be here, Mrs. Carney. Cole wrote about you in his letters."

"No, dear, please call me Evelyn. I've waited too long for a daughter-in-law to waste time being formal. Heavens, I thought neither one of my sons would ever get married."

"Th-thank you. But we're not married yet." Jodie tried to catch her breath. Evelyn Carney crackled with bustling energy and good humor. She was surprisingly youthful, with just a few threads of silver in her brown hair and a fan of laugh lines at the corners of her eyes.

"But you will be, very soon. And I can't wait to meet your children," Evelyn said happily. She opened the Jeep's door. "Aren't you a darling?" She lifted Penny and held a hand out to Tadd. "And goodness, you're so grown-up and handsome, young man."

The genuine warmth and friendliness in her voice broke through Tadd's usual reserve and he puffed with pride. "I'm eight."

"That old? But you still like peanut butter cookies, right?"

Tadd nodded quickly.

"Oh, good. Because I have a whole plateful inside, along with a big pot of cocoa. I've always wanted a couple of grandchildren to spoil. Now I get my chance."

Jodie watched bemused as Evelyn Carney disappeared into the house with Penny and Tadd. A warm hand at the small of her back made her jump.

"Mom does that," Donovan murmured. His eyes, so much like his mother's, were filled with affection. "I told you she loves kids."

"Yes. She's wonderful." Jodie caught her lower lip between her teeth and dealt with a nagging stab of guilt. Evelyn had greeted her affectionately, but what would she think if she knew her much-anticipated daughter-in-law was already having doubts whether a marriage would take place?

Not that anything was decided. She couldn't decide anything until Cole had finished his climb and she met him. But the climbing? She'd never feel comfortable about something so dangerous. On the other hand, maybe things could work out if Cole honestly intended to give it up.

"Cole said this would be his last chance to climb McKinley?" she asked, needing some kind of reassurance.

Donovan dropped his hand. "I got the impression he didn't think it was a proper hobby for a married man," he said carefully.

"It isn't." Without intending it, the words came out harsh, almost angry. Closing her eyes for an instant, Jodie took several deep breaths.

She wished she could explain she wasn't angry with Cole, she was angry with herself. She'd married a man who cared more about going supersonic in his jets than being a family man. As a result, her children didn't have their father, and that was the hardest part about losing Mark.

"Well," she said finally, "I'd better go inside and make sure your mother doesn't spoil Tadd and Penny too much. They aren't used to doting grandparent types."

"If you think my mom is bad, just wait until Shamus gets home."

"Oh?" Jodie lifted her eyebrows as they climbed the steps to the porch.

"Yup. Shamus never had kids of his own, so he's just as eager for grandkids as Mom."

"You sound fond of him."

Donovan paused. He'd never thought of it that way. Shamus Carney had always been somebody his mother cared about, someone who made her happy after years of being alone. "He's all right."

Jodie shook her head and stepped through the door he was holding for her. "Would it kill you to admit you like him?"

"Of course I like him."

She shook her head again. Men had trouble expressing their feelings—at least the men she'd grown up with. It didn't surprise her to discover Donovan had the same trouble.

Inside, Evelyn looked up with a pleased smile. "Donovan, give Jodie a tour of the house. I want you to feel right at home, Jodie. Shamus and I couldn't be happier to have you.''

"Thank you."

"See? Didn't I tell you?'' Donovan whispered as they left the kitchen. "Mom lives for company.''

The interior of the house was just as warm and welcoming as Evelyn herself. A number of bed-rooms were in the back and on a second floor, but the front half was a large, unbroken space of wood and light, with high windows that encompassed the valley and mountains beyond. Colorful braided rugs were scattered on the polished oak floor, and native art accented the walls.

"That's a Tlingit mask, right?'' she asked, gazing at a rather fierce woodcarving over the couch.

Donovan blinked. Not only had Jodie correctly identified the cultural artisan, she'd used the proper pronunciation. "I guess you *did* live in Alaska.''

"You didn't believe me?'' Her hand trailed across the pattern of a Chilkat blanket hanging on another wall. She turned and looked at him with an odd intensity in her slender body. "Did you ever feel there was a place that waited for you, a place where your soul belonged, even when you were thousands of miles away? A place where the north winds call your name.''

The last was said so softly, Donovan barely heard, yet his scalp tightened in primitive response. It was as if she'd reached inside and opened a part of him he didn't know existed. He'd traveled, sometimes for pleasure, sometimes for business, but Alaska was in his blood. It was, indeed, as though the north winds called his name.

"Never mind.'' Jodie looked flustered. "I get carried away. Too poetic—at least that's what my father used to say.''

"I don't agree," Donovan said simply. "Not everyone hears Alaska calling. I'm glad you do."

Her smile took his breath away. "Even if I don't marry Cole, I'm glad we came."

Alarm and his growing sense of guilt drove other thoughts from Donovan's head. "Even if you don't marry Cole? You've changed your mind?"

Jodie shrugged. "You have to admit this isn't the most promising beginning."

"It's just a...a..." Donovan thought furiously, trying to think of something that would keep Jodie from dumping his brother before she'd ever met him. Even if he didn't agree with this marriage, he didn't want to ruin things for Cole.

"It's a what?"

"It's just a temporary condition," he muttered finally. "Maybe it's even good. You can see Fairbanks and get acquainted with the family without any distractions." Even as the words left his mouth, he silently groaned.

Jodie laughed. "Right. Every marriage should begin without the distraction of a groom."

"Okay, you got me. You now know the Masters family secret—we have incurable foot-in-mouth disease. Mom?" he called. "Come rescue your son."

Come rescue *both* your sons.

Evelyn had been ecstatic that Cole was considering marriage. And when Donovan had called from his cell phone to let her know about the children, she'd gotten more excited than ever. It didn't matter that it was a mail-order marriage—she felt her sons were irresistible, and that any woman alive would fall in love with them.

His mother came out of the kitchen, smiling. "Is Donovan being difficult?" she asked Jodie. "You have to forgive him. He means well."

"He's relatively harmless," Jodie said. "I've just been admiring your home. It's lovely."

Evelyn beamed. "And I've been admiring your children. Penny is the sweetest thing, and Tadd is so smart. You must be proud of them."

A faint, pleased blush colored Jodie's cheeks as she nodded. Donovan sat back in a chair, trying to decide why she was so damned attractive to him. He'd always avoided dating women with children. Somehow it didn't seem right to have casual affairs with single mothers—sort of disrespectful, and certainly ripe for disaster. It might be different if he wanted to get married, but he didn't.

"Daddy, cookie?" asked Penny's voice next to him. She held out the cookie, bits of it crumbling away between her fingers.

"Oh, dear," Jodie said, hurrying to her daughter. "You're making a mess, munchkin. We'd better clean you up."

"It's all right, she won't hurt anything," Evelyn called, but Jodie had already swept Penny up and was disappearing into the kitchen. When the door had swung closed, Evelyn looked at her son and raised an eyebrow. "Daddy?"

He squirmed under her questioning gaze. "It's a misunderstanding, that's all."

"A big misunderstanding. In case you've forgotten, your rank in this arrangement is 'Uncle,' not 'Daddy.'"

Donovan agreed; he just didn't know how to repair matters. "Jodie tried to explain it to Penny, but she just assumed I was going to be her new daddy...and for a little angel she's remarkably stubborn."

"She *is* an angel," Evelyn agreed thoughtfully. "And I like Jodie, too, don't you?"

"Yeah." Donovan shot to his feet and paced the room. "She's okay. Look, I've been thinking I'll head back home to Kachelak. You and Shamus can show Jodie and the kids around Fairbanks, and I'll get back to work."

"Certainly not. You're going to stay right here and get acquainted with your new sister-in-law. Besides, you can work out of your Fairbanks office. You've done it before."

He turned and looked at his mother. "She isn't my sister-in-law yet. And it's not as convenient to work up here. It's easier in Kachelak."

"But you were coming up in a few days anyway," she said stubbornly, "along with Mike and Ross and their families for the Golden Days celebration. You know, it's been so nice since they got married—they're all so happy together," she murmured as though it was an entirely new thought, which it wasn't. She played hostess to his partners on a regular basis and often urged her eldest son to find a "nice wife" of his own.

"Don't," Donovan warned.

"Don't what, dear?"

"Don't start in on the joys of marriage." He usually laughed off her matchmaking efforts, but not today.

His mother's smile was edged with mischief. "What's wrong with marriage?"

"Of anyone, you ought to know," he said tightly.

Most of the time Donovan didn't think about the way his father had walked out, leaving a wife and two young boys to fend for themselves. It was harder to forget his mother struggling to clothe and feed them, not knowing what had happened to her husband, much less getting any support from him.

"Are you still that bitter?" Evelyn asked, her smile fading. "I'm not. I don't think I ever was."

"You were too exhausted to be bitter. Marriage is too much of a crapshoot to be worth the chance. I don't know what Cole is thinking about, much less going about it in such a cockeyed way." Donovan resumed his pacing, consumed by a restless energy he didn't understand. "For God's sake, it's a mail-order marriage."

"Not exactly. I know that's what he calls it, but he's friends with Jodie's brother. Cole said that David talked about her all the time, and after a while he got curious."

"You don't propose out of curiosity."

Evelyn sat on the couch and watched her eldest son pace. "Cole doesn't feel the way you do about marriage. And now he's the odd man out. One by one his friends here in Fairbanks have all gotten married and are starting their families. I think it's why he bought the house, instead of staying in that tiny apartment. He's lonely, Donovan."

"Tell him to get a dog."

She laughed softly. "I don't think it's that kind of lonely."

* * *

In the kitchen Jodie heard enough of the conversation between mother and son to wish she were on a different planet. Donovan thought she was "okay," but that his brother was crazy to marry her.

It hurt, though she didn't understand why. Donovan was a stranger. His opinion shouldn't count. Besides, she'd expected some resistance to the idea, especially since her own family—with the exception of David—thought it was crazy, too. She supposed Cole's family had even more to worry about than she did. Jodie Richards was a mystery to them, an unknown woman who'd suddenly appeared, bringing two children with her.

At least *she* had her brother's friendship with Cole to trust. And her father had investigated Cole with the zeal only a two-star general could muster. If Cole or his family had any unsavory secrets, Thaddeus McBride would have uncovered them in short order.

She glanced at Penny and Tadd. They were absorbed in playing with a litter of kittens, though they probably wouldn't understand what Donovan had said, even if they'd heard him.

Silently Jodie rinsed the cloth she'd used to clean Penny's face and fingers. There were cookie crumbs to clean up from the floor. If these people were going to become family, they'd have to accept her the way she was.

Even Donovan Masters.

Chapter Three

"Is something wrong, dear?" Evelyn asked, a concerned look on her face. "You seem quiet."

"No, I'm fine."

Jodie put the potato she'd been peeling into a pot and started working on another. It had been several hours since she'd heard Donovan's biting remarks about marriage, and she was more confused than ever. He'd practically demanded she stay in Alaska and wait for Cole, but he thought his brother was making a mistake.

And men said women were illogical.

"Are you sure?" Evelyn urged. "There's time to lie down before dinner."

Jodie forced a smile to her face and shook her head. "Please don't worry. I'm a little over-whelmed, that's all. It's been a big day."

"You mean, expecting Cole and getting the rest of us instead?"

The older woman's perception caught Jodie by

surprise. Since her own mother had died she'd been surrounded by men—her brothers, her father and later her husband. None of them had been notably insightful.

"How much did Cole tell you about me?" Jodie asked, rather than wandering into dangerous territory. She didn't want to admit she'd accidentally overheard Evelyn's earlier conversation with Donovan.

"Mostly that you were beautiful and intelligent and that you loved Alaska. It was more than enough."

"Okay, *when* did he tell you about me?" Jodie countered dryly.

Evelyn laughed. "I didn't know he'd proposed until a couple of days ago, but don't worry about that. He probably wanted to be sure you were really coming before getting my hopes up."

"Of course." Jodie dropped another potato into the pot. "Is that enough, or do we need more?"

"Enough," Evelyn pronounced. "Even for that big Irishman I married."

The palpable love in her voice tore at Jodie. She'd once wanted that kind of love for herself—she'd even had it for a time. Now all she wanted was something safe and predictable. In the bottom of her heart she suspected it was a form of cowardice, but it was a cowardice she couldn't seem to overcome.

"What's that about me bein' big?"

Shamus Carney stood at the doorway, or rather, he *filled* the doorway. None of him was fat, it was simply the height and muscle and square dimensions of a large, well-built man. He'd changed from his suit since arriving home, but he still looked like a successful oil executive…with touches of silver-haired teddy bear.

"Now, Evie darlin', you know we leave the really big ones at home," Shamus continued in his lingering Irish brogue. "I'm barely keeper size."

"Better than keeper size," Evelyn murmured. A private look was exchanged between husband and wife, a look of loving promises made and kept.

Donovan stood nearby, his hands thrust into his pockets. The contrast between the two men couldn't have been more obvious. For all his size, Shamus dressed and *looked* like what he was, a high-powered executive. But Donovan… Jodie glanced at him again from the corner of her eye, trying to decide what category he fit into.

Tall and trim, with a strong body that suggested he was accustomed to hard work. But it wasn't his muscles that were so appealing to watch, it was the way he moved with a comfortable, masculine grace. He was adequately covered by worn jeans, a blue flannel shirt neatly tucked into those jeans and a black T-shirt beneath, yet he still made her mouth go dry.

Stop.

Jodie threw on her mental brakes with an effort. She'd been in a sexual deep freeze for so long that she'd lost all perspective. Donovan was a man—that was enough of a category. She shouldn't think about him any more than necessary.

"Mom," Donovan said, flicking Jodie a look. "Got some lemonade? We're going to cut some winter firewood, so we'll get thirsty fast."

"You shouldn't work so hard. You're visiting," Evelyn objected. "Talk to him, Shamus."

"I have, darlin', but you've a hardheaded son."

"I get it from my mother," Donovan countered, a smile playing on his lips.

Everything was said in a fond, comfortable way. They'd probably had this discussion a hundred times, and would have it a hundred more. Threads of regret slid through Jodie. Her mother had been the one who held things together, the one who softened the general's hard edges. Jodie had tried, but the loss of his wife had damaged Thaddeus McBride, leaving wounds through his soul that never seemed to heal.

She didn't want to be like that. Not anymore. She needed to protect herself, but that didn't mean she had to retreat from life. Becoming part of this loving family was fast becoming an important element of her plan to marry Cole.

"I've never seen anyone chop wood," Jodie said. "Mind if I watch?"

"That t'would be a real pleasure, Jodie love." Shamus's smile gentled. Upon learning her maiden name of McBride, he'd instantly pronounced Jodie a girl from the Emerald Isle, though she'd protested that her Irish roots were diluted and generations back.

"I should learn something useful about living in Alaska. Maybe you could teach me how to use that ax," she suggested.

A look of alarm froze both men's faces.

"I'm sure Cole will split any wood that needs to be cut," Donovan said quickly.

"I should still know how—"

"Change into something more practical, then we'll talk about it." Turning on his heel, he headed out the back door. Shamus followed, his expression as perplexed as his wife's.

Jodie self-consciously smoothed the sleeve of her silk blouse. In a world of jeans and flannel, she probably *did* look impractical.

Evelyn patted her hand. "Don't let him trouble you. Shamus won't let me cut wood, either—men are like that the world over." She shrugged. "And Donovan has always been too protective. He just doesn't want you to get hurt when he feels responsible for your safety."

It was more than that, but Jodie kept her mouth shut. Underlying Donovan's outward friendliness, was an edge of disapproval; he was convinced she wasn't the right woman for his brother.

"Well, I'll see if the children are still napping, then change my clothes," she said, rising. "Unless I can help more with dinner?"

"Go on, dear. I have things in hand."

Jodie headed for the back of the house, mentally reviewing her limited travel wardrobe. She hadn't come prepared to brave the wilderness; she'd come for a summer visit. With all of Tadd and Penny's things to pack, as well, she'd opted mostly for light blouses, shorts, a couple pairs of jeans and a few T-shirts. They took the least space in a suitcase.

Sighing, Jodie took out a pair of jeans and a pink T-shirt. If Donovan didn't like her clothing, then too bad.

Donovan brought the head of the maul down on the last wedge, splitting the log into two clean pieces. He sensed Shamus's puzzled gaze, even as they worked in tandem on the familiar chore of preparing for a northern winter. It was something that began each spring as soon as the landscape eased from the grip of the cold and ice.

"You were rude, lad," Shamus finally said softly.

Donovan flicked a glance at his mother's husband and shifted uncomfortably. The quiet rebuke was the closest the elder man had ever come to sounding like a dad. Shamus had never acted like a father because, quite simply, Donovan had never let him get that close.

You sound fond of him.

The memory of Jodie's astute observation gave Donovan a queer sensation in his chest. He suddenly knew that Shamus had wanted to be a father, but he'd barely been allowed friendship.

"You're right. I'll apologize," he said.

"Why?"

Donovan knew the question wasn't why should he apologize, but why he'd acted like a jackass. Beneath Shamus's Irish congeniality was a shrewd man, in both the business world, and the business of people.

Why?

Because I can't help seeing Jodie as a woman, not as a sister-in-law.

Setting the maul on the ground, Donovan lifted another log to the chopping block. Shamus still waited for the answer, but it wasn't something Donovan wanted to admit out loud.

"She's a fine woman, lad," Shamus said, breaking the silence. "You can see it in her eyes, and in her children. The same way you can see it in your mother."

The oblique compliment unexpectedly warmed

Donovan. He'd always thought he didn't need a father's approval. His own father's opinion certainly
wasn't worth caring about, yet all at once it meant
a lot that Shamus thought he measured up, at least
in some things.

"Jodie...disturbs me," Donovan admitted, relieved to let it out. "She isn't what I expected."

"Few women are."

He grabbed the maul again. "And she's planning
to marry Cole."

"Aye, that is a trouble."

The economy of words was enough, Donovan
could tell Shamus understood his dilemma. In a
small way it eased some of the tension gripping him.

The sound of a door opening and closing drew
their attention, and Donovan's breath hissed out at
the sight of Jodie, dressed in close-fitting black jeans
and a T-shirt, carrying a tray with two ice-filled
glasses. The soft pink fabric clung to her breasts,
emphasizing both their sweet roundness and her
slender waist below.

Donovan's fingers clenched around the wood handle of the maul and he mentally counted the days
until Cole would return home. He knew the statis-
tics; a climb up Mount McKinley's West Buttress
took an average of nineteen to twenty-one days.

Might as well be a lifetime.

"Is this more practical?" Jodie murmured.

"You look just fine," Shamus said. "But then,
you were always fine. Isn't that right, Donovan?"

"Yeah," he muttered, then shook himself. "I
didn't mean to be rude."

She smiled, though it didn't quite reach her eyes.

"That's all right. It's been a strange day for all of us."

"You're a kind one, Jodie love." Shamus smiled and took the tray she carried. He put it on a stump and motioned to an Adirondack chair, well away from the possibility of flying wood chips. "Watch and you'll see some fancy cuttin'."

Jodie sank into the chair and watched the two men work. Shamus had a broader shoulder span, and he brought the ax down with a crack of blunt strength. But Donovan...He worked with a coordinated power that sent more uncomfortable sensations into her abdomen.

She shivered in the cool air. Though she knew Fairbanks could get fairly warm in the summer, this wasn't a warm day, particularly after the heat and humidity of Florida.

The brush of a demanding paw on her leg was a welcome distraction, and she looked down at a half-grown husky pup. "Aren't you a beauty?" she said.

The puppy rose on his hind legs and clambered into her lap, yipping with excitement. His thick pelt of black-tipped silver fur drew her fingers like a magnet, and she stroked him with increasing fascination. Across the yard an adult husky sat with grave dignity. Two more pups played at her side, rolling around on the ground with the exuberance of youth.

Pausing to stack the wood they'd cut so far, Donovan watched dog and woman.

"Looks like Klondike has adopted her," Shamus murmured. He, too, had stopped, his attention drawn by Jodie's quiet laughter and her sensuous appreciation of the animal.

"Isn't he the one you said was standoffish?"

asked Donovan, who hadn't been in Fairbanks since before the pups were born. The summer was his company's busiest time, keeping everyone at Triple M Transit racing to keep up with the pace. He and his partners only took one break the entire time, when they came to Fairbanks for the summer festival.

"He's always been a loner, but he seems to have taken to Jodie right off," Shamus said, watching woman and puppy with fond approval.

Donovan couldn't help himself, he walked across the yard and gave Klondike's velvety ears a rub. But he regretted the impulsive action when Jodie's chuckles ceased. Was she remembering his thoughtless words in the kitchen? He'd been rude out of frustration with his own feelings, not for anything she'd said or done.

"Shamus told me about this puppy," Donovan said, crouching next to the chair. "Klondike is very selective about the people he cozies up to. Seems he approves of you, though."

"But you don't." Jodie couldn't believe her wayward tongue and fought to keep embarrassed heat from flooding her fair skin. "Never mind," she added swiftly. "We just have to get used to each other, that's all."

"Right." His eyes were unreadable.

"Daddy," called a persistent voice, breaking the moment. "I waked up."

They groaned simultaneously.

"I don't know how I'm going to explain this to Cole," Donovan said, even as he opened his arms to accept Penny's enthused hug. "I really don't."

Jodie didn't know, either. She'd had a long talk

with Penny before her nap. Her daughter had nodded solemnly as her mother explained that Donovan *wasn't* her daddy, he was Uncle Donovan. She should have known the resolute core in Penny's nature wouldn't give up so easily.

She wanted Donovan to be her daddy.

It was that simple.

But as the hard strength of his arm brushed hers, Jodie knew things were getting more complicated than she'd ever thought possible.

It was after one in the morning when Jodie kicked the blankets away. She couldn't sleep. Her body was still on Florida time. Only, it wasn't really the time difference keeping her awake, it was the chaos in her mind.

Klondike lifted his head from a rug on the floor and whined softly.

"Don't mind me, little one." She knelt and rubbed his fur, seeking his eager warmth beneath her fingers. The Carneys had happily said to keep the husky pup with her, dropping deliberate hints about making him a gift.

It was a generous offer. Jodie had learned that Shamus Carney raised champion sled dogs, and was himself an ardent participant in the various Alaskan mushing events like the Yukon Quest and Iditarod sled dog races. The Yukon Quest was one thousand miles of grueling ice and work and winter storms, covering some of the roughest territory in Alaska. At eleven hundred miles, the Iditarod wasn't any better.

Or safer.

Irritably Jodie straightened and yanked a robe

over her shoulders. Did everyone in this family need dangerous outlets for their energy? Didn't life have enough challenges and danger and risk without voluntarily jumping over a cliff?

Jodie wandered into the living room, then stepped out onto the porch with Klondike padding at her heels.

It wasn't dark. With less than three hours between sunrise and sunset during Fairbanks' summer, there wasn't time for it to get dark. The twilight was peaceful though, a period of quiet during the brief, frantic growing season of the northern lands.

Snow-covered mountains rested blue and serene on the horizon, a hazy band of darker blue and purple separating them from the earth. They floated like surreal clouds, their saw-toothed peaks catching the first rays of the rising sun...sunrise at two in the morning. Jodie leaned her arms on the railing, staring into the distance.

"You're a long way away," Donovan said softly from the end of the porch.

Somehow, Jodie wasn't surprised to find him awake and seeking a moment of peace.

"Just admiring...*this*," she answered, throwing her hand out to encompass the shadowed birch and aspen forest below, along with the startling beauty of the Alaska Range. "That's where Mount McKinley is, isn't it?"

"Yeah." Donovan stood next to her, shattering what little tranquillity she'd managed to achieve.

Jodie tried to think about Cole, climbing in the ice and snow, but he was just an abstract, while his brother was very real and alive, and so close, she could feel the warmth of his body.

"A lot of Alaskans called it Denali," Donovan murmured. He closed his eyes, shutting out the blue-white mountains that taunted his conscience.

"Denali?" Jodie turned toward him. "That's right. I'd forgotten."

"It's an Athabascan word. It means the 'high one.'"

"And Alyeska is the 'great land.'" The Aleut word rolled musically from her mouth. "I do remember that much," she added softly.

Donovan drew a deep breath. A mistake, because it filled his senses with Jodie's uniquely feminine scent.

"Look, about what you said earlier...about me not approving of you," he whispered.

"No, I shouldn't have said anything." Jodie shook her head, her unbound hair sliding across her shoulders and brushing his arm. It was like cool fire on his skin, silk and flame in the gathering light.

"It isn't you, Jodie."

"Of course not."

How did a man explain that he was sexually attracted to a woman, but he was honor-bound to keep his hands to himself? He could come right out and say the words, but Donovan had an idea that Jodie would be annoyed. Most women didn't appreciate an honest declaration of desire, not unless it was accompanied by a declaration of love. Yet it was more than that. If he put those feelings into words, they would become too real, too inescapable.

"Why does Cole's climbing bother you so much?" Donovan asked instead, though he suspected climbing was a risky subject, as well.

Jodie was silent for so long, he didn't think she

would answer, then a sigh eased from her chest. She sank bonelessly to the deck and gathered Klondike into her arms. The pup was quiet, sensitive to the moods of the human he'd chosen. And he *had* chosen Jodie. His attachment to her became stronger with each passing hour.

"Cole is risking his life for nothing," she said without looking up. "There's no reason to climb McKinley. Nobody's life needs saving. There's no scientific value in it. It's just something he wants to do."

Donovan whistled softly, wondering what Jodie would say if she knew that both he and Cole participated in the annual Arctic Man Ski and Snow-Go Classic, known to some insiders as the "Ski to Die" race. Or of the times they'd camped in the wilderness, once playing dead while a grizzly bear pawed at them. Or that Cole shared his stepfather's passion for mushing and planned to compete in the Iditarod next year. He was so competitive, he'd probably win the race, too.

Plainly, there were a few things Cole *hadn't* shared in his letters, things that might have affected Jodie's decision to come to Alaska. But even if his brother hadn't been entirely forthright, Donovan couldn't say anything. Those truths needed to come from Cole.

Donovan sat next to Jodie and leaned against the slatted rails. It was a relief to turn his back on the mountains, to shut out their subtle reminders of guilt and honor.

"Cole should have told me about the climbing," Jodie said in the silence.

"Would you have still come if he had?"

After another long wait she sighed. "I—I don't know. Probably not."

Maybe that's why he didn't tell you, Donovan thought, but he didn't say it aloud, instead watching Jodie as she cuddled Klondike to her. The haunting, wild cry of a loon echoed through the air and her face became peaceful. Her body swayed in the cool breezes sweeping across the porch, at one with the surrounding world.

He didn't doubt she was listening once again to the call of the north winds. She had an acceptance of Alaska's wildness, greater than that of any woman he'd known. So why didn't she accept Cole's need to meet one of its great challenges?

"That pup," Donovan whispered. "He'll grow into more than fifty pounds of muscle and teeth and instinct, held back by his love for a human. He's got some husky, shepherd, even a few drops of wolf blood. You accept him. Why not Cole's climbing?"

She hugged Klondike closer to her. "People are different. They can choose, and sometimes they choose things that get them killed. It would be different if Cole was just a friend who climbed as a hobby, but we're supposed to get married."

"People can get hurt anywhere, anytime," Donovan murmured. "Just walking across a street or getting into a car. Nobody is perfectly safe, whether they're in a city, or on top of a mountain."

"You're right, but the odds are better if you don't go out looking for trouble. Believe it or not, I *do* understand why Cole is climbing that mountain. But my children have already lost one father," Jodie said quietly. "I don't want them to lose another."

The impact of her words hit Donovan like a blow,

and he pulled a harsh breath into his lungs. Jodie wasn't a divorcée in search of a new life, she was a woman whose husband had died. It changed things.

"What happened?"

There was another long wait.

"Mark was an air force pilot," she said at last. "A hotshot, leaving vapor trails whether he was on the ground or in the air."

The anger and pain in Jodie's voice made Donovan clench his hands to keep from touching her. He wanted to believe he'd comfort anyone hurting—that it had nothing to do with her being beautiful and soft—but he couldn't be sure. He was having too much trouble keeping his hands off Jodie to trust his motives.

"Mark took a lot of chances...*unnecessary* chances," she continued. "He was killed two and a half years ago in a training flight."

Donovan did some swift math in his head and realized she must have been pregnant when her husband was killed. "Then Penny...?"

"That's right," Jodie murmured, guessing his thoughts. "I was five months along, and already having some trouble from anemia. Mark had just been posted to Turkey and I was alone there with Tadd." She stroked her stomach with a restless hand. "By the time my father arrived, I was in the base hospital, desperately trying to keep from losing the pregnancy."

"From what you've said about General McBride, I imagine he wasn't much comfort."

She looked at Donovan, knowing he'd gotten a poor impression of her father. For some reason it was important that Donovan understand. General Thaddeus McBride was a flawed man, but he loved his family and was fiercely determined to do right by them.

Jodie shook her head. "You're wrong. He brought in the best obstetric specialists he could find, Donovan. He stayed with me every minute, taking care of everything that needed to be done, and when I was stronger he brought us home to the States. If it hadn't been for my father, I wouldn't have Penny now."

Tears swam in Jodie's eyes, as they did every time she remembered how close she'd come to losing her daughter. Penny, who brightened each day with her bright smile and sunny temperament.

Donovan waited, then asked one of the questions plaguing him. "But you're determined to get married in a place that's thousands of miles away from him. Why? It isn't as if you're in love with Cole—you've never even met him."

She shrugged, and he sensed her withdrawal as clearly as if she'd put up a wall. "I told you how I felt about Alaska. And marrying Cole makes sense. We have a lot of common interests."

Jodie might love Alaska and have an instinct for the land, but Donovan wondered if she was really prepared to live there. She wanted things to be safe. While Alaska was many extraordinary things, it wasn't safe, not if you wanted to explore the land and feel its textures.

And along with all his other answered questions, Donovan started to wonder what Jodie wanted to feel.

Or if she wanted to feel anything at all.

Chapter Four

Donovan's head hurt and he pushed his face deeper in his pillow. He was reluctant to surrender the few minutes of sleep he'd finally gotten. If he tried really hard, he might be able to drop off again.

Pat, pat, pat.

What?

Donovan lifted his face and stared at the gray cat patting his aching scalp with a determined paw.

"What do you want, Buzbee?"

"Meorrw." She butted his forehead with her head and a purr vibrated from her chest.

Tarnation. He'd forgotten Buzbee's unique talent for opening doors. She had a feline's curiosity to the nth degree, and she was extremely social. It wasn't unusual to wake up in the morning and discover every bedroom door in the house ajar. Privacy wasn't something Buzbee considered a priority, which was the reason all the bedroom doors also had hook locks to circumvent her special talent.

He gave the cat a stroke down her back and a scratch on the neck and she purred louder.

The house was quiet except for someone moving around in the kitchen. Probably his mother, getting up early to prepare the kind of breakfast she considered appropriate for a prospective daughter-in-law. He figured Evelyn Carney would get along with any woman Cole planned to marry, but she seemed to truly enjoy Jodie's company.

With a sigh he climbed out of bed and pulled a pair of jeans over his legs. Right now he needed coffee—hot and strong and with the uncompromising kick of a mule.

His mother looked up from the stove as he stumbled into the kitchen and smiled. "Didn't you get any sleep?" she asked.

"At least five minutes worth."

Her smile faded as she pulled a mug from the cupboard. "Does the thought of Cole getting married really bother you so much?"

No, *Jodie* bothers me, Donovan thought silently.

Sure, he had a problem with Cole getting married, but it was his brother's decision. Mostly it was the way *he* felt around Jodie. He couldn't remember the last time a woman had gotten under his skin so badly.

As a pilot he'd developed an instinct for hazardous situations, and something about Jodie Richards screamed *caution* in a way he couldn't ignore.

"I don't...I guess it's Cole's business," Donovan muttered finally. "But he needs to be careful, be sure it's going to work out with Jodie before they get married. She's right. It isn't fair to Tadd and Penny for them to lose another father."

"Another father?" Evelyn turned around. "She didn't say anything about this last night. When did you discuss the children's father with Jodie?"

Donovan winced. "Well, she had trouble sleeping, too. We talked for a while. Her husband died in an accident while she was expecting Penny."

Evelyn made a soft, distressed sound. "That poor child."

He didn't know if she meant Jodie, or Penny, or both. Jodie and her children had gone through rough times, and the pain in her voice still echoed in his mind. Loss was loss, whether it was from a father walking out on his family, or going down in a plane.

Love made you vulnerable. If you had to get married, maybe a mail-order marriage was the best idea. That way your heart wasn't involved, which seemed to be exactly what Jodie wanted. A sensible, businesslike arrangement.

"Son?"

Donovan looked up, realizing his mother had been trying to get his attention. "Yes?"

"I just said that it's going to be so much fun once your friends get here. Ross and Mike married such lovely women, and the children are a delight."

"Right." Donovan hid a grin at his mother's obvious excitement. Evelyn and Shamus Carney were never happier than when they had a houseful of people to fuss over, especially if some of them were kids. He should be grateful to his two partners for providing surrogate grandchildren for his mother and stepfather.

"Can you believe Hannah said they shouldn't stay here because of the baby crying at night?" Evelyn asked, shaking her head while she stirred blueberry pancake batter. "I told her we wouldn't hear of it, and that Shamus and I would take care of little Mary so they could get some sleep. New parents never get enough rest."

"Little Mary?" asked Jodie from the door.

Her face was soft with sleep and the sight made Donovan shift uncomfortably. He deliberately shifted his gaze, but not before he'd also seen how her shirt clung to her body, and the way her shorts revealed sleek, tanned legs.

It didn't help to remind himself about Cole, and he wondered what it would be like to spend his life desiring his brother's wife. The prospect wasn't appealing.

Evelyn cast a smile at the younger woman. "Mary is Ross and Hannah McCoy's new baby. They also have a boy, who's seven. They're coming to Fairbanks in a few days, along with Mike and Callie and their two sons for the Golden Days celebration. Ross and Mike are Donovan's partners in his air-transit business," she added.

"Oh." Jodie smoothed her fingers across the cuff of her shorts, suddenly seeming nervous. "That's a lot of company. Maybe I should take Tadd and Penny to a motel."

"You won't do any such thing." Evelyn looked alarmed at the suggestion. "We have plenty of room."

"Well—"

"Tell her, Donovan. That's why we have such a big house—so everyone can stay over."

Donovan laughed at his mother's consternation. She plainly didn't intend to let Jodie out of her sight until she was safely married to Cole. Evelyn had waited too long for a daughter-in-law and grand-children to let such promising candidates escape.

"I told you, Mom loves having folks here," he said. He rose and held a chair for Jodie. She slid into it without looking at him. Had she slept better than he'd managed? From the faint shadows beneath her eyes he doubted it.

Buzbee brushed against his leg crying plaintively, so he picked her up and arranged her against his bare chest. For a minute he considered putting on a shirt, then decided Jodie didn't look shocked at his attire. If she'd grown up with all those brothers, she must be accustomed to men without shirts.

"How many brothers did you say you had?" he asked.

"Four. All older."

"You'll have plenty to talk about with Hannah," Donovan said, smiling at Jodie's faintly exasperated tone. "She raised six younger brothers."

"Six?" Jodie blinked and thought Hannah must have more patience than a saint. She accepted the cup of coffee Evelyn slid in front of her and looked surreptitiously at Donovan leaning back in his chair. The cat he held purred in lazy contentment, obviously delighted with her accommodations.

Jodie took a quick sip of the coffee and tried not to envy the feline. She wasn't an impressionable teenager, unable to control her hormones at the sight of well-developed pectoral muscles. She was a woman with two children and years of dealing with the opposite sex.

Yet somehow that didn't keep her from wanting to touch Donovan's hard chest and test the strength of those muscles for herself. He wasn't furry like some men; a narrow wedge of brown hair arrowed down to his waist, but the rest of him was smooth, tanned skin stretched over masculine planes.

"I...uh, I'm glad I let Klondike out earlier. If that cat gets startled, your chest will look like a dartboard," she said, then mentally groaned. She shouldn't have said anything, especially something that showed she'd noticed his body. She was cracked; it was the only explanation.

Donovan lifted an eyebrow. "Buzbee's pretty mellow. I think my chest is safe."

"Put on a shirt, son," Evelyn scolded. "You'll have Jodie thinking we're barbarians."

"Really? Do you think we're barbarians, Jodie?" he asked.

Jodie shook her head, keeping a warm flush from her cheeks with an effort. Donovan's frank teasing was something new in her experience. He seemed to take life at an easy pace, enjoying himself without fuss or making things too complicated. After living with her father, whose idea of relaxation was a formal dinner at the officers' club, she found it unexpectedly appealing.

"By the way," Donovan murmured, "in case Mom didn't already tell you, Buzbee is a door opener. So if you didn't put the hook on, and your bedroom was open this morning, it's her fault—cats think a closed door is an insult."

"That's all right, I don't sleep in the..." Jodie's words trailed, and this time she couldn't control the pink color flooding her cheeks.

I don't sleep in the nude.

She'd almost said it. Not that there was anything *wrong* with sleeping in the nude, or *not* sleeping that way. But just the thought of being naked in the same house with Donovan Masters made her uncomfortable in a very feminine way. She was much too aware of Donovan for her own good.

Amused devilment lurked in Donovan's brown eyes and Jodie curled her fingers. He knew what she'd almost slipped saying, and if they'd been alone he would have pursued the subject.

And it was her own fault, she'd started it by mentioning his chest...his *bare* chest.

Think about Cole.

Yeah, that was good advice. She didn't want to notice Donovan. If she married Cole, Donovan would be her brother-in-law. Thank heavens he lived south of Anchorage, several hundred miles away. It could be awkward if he lived in Fairbanks and she had to see him very often.

"Er...may I help with breakfast?" Jodie asked brightly, deliberately looking at Evelyn.

"Certainly not. You just sit and relax. We're going to have a busy day—the World Eskimo-Indian Olympics are being held this week, and they're having the blanket toss today. Tadd and Penny will love seeing that. Tell her about it, son."

"Sure...the blanket toss," Donovan said, the smile deepening in his eyes. "It's a group activity."

Group activity? If she could have gotten away with it, Jodie would have strangled him. She knew there really *was* an Alaskan event called a blanket toss, but Donovan's grin suggested he wasn't talking about an Eskimo sport. He wasn't even flirting, just teasing to see her blush.

"I know all about the blanket toss," Jodie returned, giving him a repressive look. How could she remember Cole if Donovan kept making her feel things she shouldn't? Things she didn't want to feel for any man.

"I hope Tadd and Penny like a big breakfast," Evelyn said, providing a moment of relief. "We can eat as soon as everyone is ready."

"They're good eaters," Jodie assured. "Especially Tadd. I'll go see if they're awake."

Feeling like a coward, Jodie escaped to the bedroom she shared with Penny. In the dresser mirror, she looked at her reflection and frowned. Beneath the cool exterior she'd cultivated was the abandoned teenager who'd fallen for a daredevil air force pilot.

Jodie smiled faintly, remembering the excitement of falling in love—blood racing in anticipation, breathless moments of exhilaration, followed by equal amounts of sheer desolation.

Lord, it had been fun.

That was the worst part about Donovan; he made her long for the days when she wasn't afraid of her own heart.

"Stop it." Jodie tapped her fingers on her thigh. She had to keep some perspective. Even if she was willing to risk her heart a second time, Donovan wasn't the marrying kind. Cole was a much safer husband prospect.

Penny sat up and sleepily rubbed her eyes. "Where, Daddy?"

"*Uncle* Donovan is in the kitchen," Jodie corrected gently. She was beginning to realize that bringing the children on this trip might have been a mistake. Tadd hated the idea of an accountant father, and Penny had stubbornly decided Donovan was her daddy.

It would have been all right if Cole hadn't gone on that blasted climb, she reminded herself.

Sighing, she helped Penny in the bathroom, then dressed her in a T-shirt and blue corduroy overalls. When freed from her mother's ministrations, the two-year-old trotted away. Though the kitchen was some distance from the bedrooms, the distinctive cry of "Daddy," could be heard a few seconds later.

Jodie leaned against the wall outside of Tadd's room and felt a headache developing.

"Don't mind it, Jodie love," said Shamus Carney's kind voice. "You'll sort it out."

She managed a smile. "Do you think Cole will be upset?"

"He's a fine lad, and not one to worry about such things. Penny will learn who to call Daddy in good time."

"It seems that she's learned it already," Jodie said dryly.

His laugh boomed out. "Being a daddy is more than a name. Cole will understand."

Cole... She tried to bring his image to mind, but Donovan's face kept interfering. Of course, they were brothers, so they looked a lot alike, she reasoned. And she'd only seen Cole's picture, she'd never met him in person.

Tadd's door opened and he walked out, dressed except for a rumpled head of hair. "Mom, I'm *starving*," he declared.

"You're always starving. Comb your hair, then you can eat."

"Aw, *Mom*."

"Hair." Jodie pointed into the bedroom and he stomped back inside. When he reappeared, his hair had been slicked into a reasonably neat semblance of order, though it always had a tendency to stick up. He dashed down the hallway as if he was truly starving, instead of suffering from a normal boy's appetite.

"You'd think he's never eaten before," Jodie muttered.

Shamus just laughed and drew her arm through his, escorting her to the kitchen with old-world courtliness.

In the sunny breakfast nook Penny insisted upon sitting on Donovan's lap. When Jodie tried to dissuade her, he said it was fine—between his two partners' families, he had experience feeding kids. But after Penny had spilled a glass of milk on his jeans and smeared apricot jam in his hair, Jodie wondered if he regretted that assurance.

Her lips twitched as he rose at the end of the meal, fruitlessly wiping a napkin over the various spills and smears.

"I'll just take a shower," Donovan murmured finally, wondering how such a small child could cause so much mess. "And change into something else." He looked at Jodie and saw she was having trouble keeping a straight face.

It served him right. He shouldn't have teased her; she probably thought this was a perfect payback. He tossed his sodden napkin in her direction.

"What does the general say about his granddaughter's table manners?" he asked.

"Penny is his one weakness," Jodie confessed. Her eyes glowed with love as she wiped her daughter's face and hands. "She can wrap him around her little finger with just a smile."

It didn't surprise Donovan. Penny had already wrapped *him* around her little finger.

"What about Tadd?" he asked, glancing out the window where Shamus and Tadd had gone to feed the husky team. "I get the impression that things are tense between them."

Jodie sighed. "Tadd is the first grandson. My father is determined to mold him into a perfect candidate for the air force academy. Funny thing is, Tadd actually wanted to be an air force pilot before his grandfather started to drill him. As much as a child wants to be anything," she added.

"A pilot like his dad?" If Donovan hadn't been watching closely, he wouldn't have seen the faint quiver that went through Jodie at the quiet comment.

"Yeah. Like his dad." Jodie kept her face averted as she collected plates and silverware together. "It isn't any surprise that Tadd wanted to be a pilot. Mark used to take him up in a private plane, teaching him to fly practically before he could walk."

Donovan knew he should take his shower and stay out of the Richards' family business, but he couldn't resist learning more. Was Jodie really over her husband's death? Would she marry Cole, thinking she wanted a marriage without love, then discover she wanted more after all?

"How did you meet Mark?" he asked softly, to keep his mom from overhearing.

"How does any officer's daughter meet an air force pilot?" Jodie smiled sadly. "We met on the base. I was a rebellious eighteen-year-old, and he was a hot-tempered lieutenant who couldn't stay out of trouble. My father didn't approve, which naturally convinced me Mark was the perfect guy."

"General McBride must have been beside himself."

Her smile turned impish, revealing small dimples at the corners of her mouth. "You have no idea."

Actually, Donovan was getting a pretty good idea of the general. Jodie loved him, but would prefer living a few thousand miles apart. It seemed clear enough.

"Are you still rebellious?" he murmured.

"Sometimes. But now I call it determination and self-reliance."

"I see."

As though uncomfortable with his direct gaze, Jodie looked down, then frowned. "I know Fairbanks isn't like Florida, but Cole told me to bring shorts to wear during the day. He said it's been an unusually warm summer so they'd be okay, even if they aren't that practical."

The change in subject surprised Donovan, but only for a moment. She obviously remembered his thoughtless comments the previous afternoon and expected him to be equally disapproving of her current attire.

"I always enjoy seeing a pretty girl in shorts," he drawled. "I'll have to thank Cole for suggesting it."

"Oh...okay."

Donovan couldn't be sure, but he thought there was a deepening of the pink in Jodie's face.

"Well," he said reluctantly, "I'd better take that shower."

He waited a moment, then left the kitchen. He needed to make a few business calls, maybe even stop in at the office. With any luck he could avoid the day with Jodie and her children altogether.

It wasn't that he didn't like them.

No. It was because he liked them entirely too much.

How the hell did this happen?

Donovan stared ahead at the road, frowning at the Dodge Durango ahead of him. Inside the other vehicle was Shamus, along with his mother and Tadd.

But not Jodie and Penny.

Jodie sat next to him, and Penny was buckled into a borrowed child's seat in the back. And instead of going to the Triple M branch office, he was headed for the World Eskimo-Indian Olympics. A day of the games, at least; the events took place over a period of four days.

"I'm sorry you got pushed into this," Jodie said quietly. "We could have fit into the other car. No matter what your mom says, it wasn't that crowded."

Donovan glanced at Jodie and sighed. Since her arrival he'd been guilty of more rude behavior than he liked to think about. And normally he would have enjoyed seeing the traditional Alaska competitions, especially with a beautiful woman at his side. He was quite fond of the opposite sex as long as they kept wedding rings out of their plans.

"Naw," he said. "Don't be silly. It's been years since I've been able to attend the games. Summer is such a busy time for the company, we don't take enough time for recreation."

"What about the Golden Days celebration? Your mother said you all come up to Fairbanks for that."

"Only for the past three years. It's Ross and Mike's idea. Things have really changed since they got married. I used to be the one who wanted to take time off, now they're the first to suggest it."

"Oh."

"We don't do as much of the flying anymore, either, so we have more time than we used to," Donovan said.

"Evelyn mentioned your business was doing well. She's very proud of you."

Jodie still sounded quiet, and guilt gnawed at Donovan for being so insensitive. This wasn't her fault. She'd come to Alaska, with every expectation of meeting Cole and deciding if they were compatible. She couldn't have known her fiancé would take off for Mount McKinley at the last minute.

She was engaged to his brother. As long as he kept that in mind, there wasn't any reason they couldn't be friends.

Right?

Something in his reasoning seemed flawed, but he wasn't in the mood to examine it. Jodie might make Cole very happy. He had to let his brother make his own decisions.

"I think we started wrong," Donovan said softly. "Let's pretend we just met, and that I never shoved my foot in my mouth."

They stopped at a traffic light and he looked at her more fully. She seemed to be considering his offer with more intensity than it deserved.

"How about it? Friends?" He held out his hand.

Jodie stared at the proffered hand. Her mind was all for being friends with Donovan, but her body wanted something else. Was it possible for them to be friends if her nerves jumped to attention each time she saw him?

Well...anything was possible.

She put her fingers in his and shook.

It was worth trying.

By the middle of the day Jodie's head was whirling with the sights and sounds of Fairbanks. The World Eskimo-Indian Olympics—or WEIO some folks called them—were more than sporting events. There were traditional dances and demonstrations, songs, storytelling and the laughter of people enjoying themselves to the fullest.

Shamus and Evelyn were determinedly keeping tabs on the children, insisting she relax and enjoy herself. It would have been a great idea except she kept getting thrown together with Donovan.

Like now.

Here she was, alone with Donovan Masters, with neither her children or the Carneys in sight. Practicing friendship was one thing, courting disaster was another.

What was it about him?

After his initial objections to attending the games with the family, he'd thrown himself into the day. He laughed often and easily, chatting comfortably with strangers and describing the practical origins behind the various events.

Not that everyone was a stranger. It seemed as if half the people participating either knew Donovan, or Shamus and Evelyn.

"How about one like this?" Donovan lifted a particularly fierce-looking Yup'ik mask. "I'll bet Tadd would like it on his wall. Guaranteed to disturb a few nights' sleep.'' He held the mask up to his face and growled.

Jodie laughed and shuddered at the same time. They'd been browsing through the booths of native arts, and each of Donovan's suggestions had been more outrageous than the last.

"Don't even think it," she ordered. "If Tadd thought you approved, he'd never let me have any peace until I got one for him. He thinks you're pretty terrific."

"That's just because I'm a pilot." Donovan sent her a teasing smile.

"Mmm." Jodie thought her son was responding to more than Donovan's career. Donovan had a casual, easy charm, and he gave Tadd just the right amount of attention to make him feel important. "Considering the way he acted at the airport yesterday, you've been very patient with him."

Donovan shrugged. "It's going to be tough for him accepting a new father. At least you don't have that problem with Penny."

"No, she just wants the wrong father," Jodie retorted. Their eyes met for an uncomfortable moment, then she looked down at the beadwork she held.

She still sensed that Donovan didn't approve of her, and it was all tangled up with the way he felt about marriage. Unfortunately she couldn't come right out and ask *why* he was against one of the world's oldest institutions.

Of course, there were more ways than one of finding out.

"Uh...tell me, why hasn't a nice guy like *you* found himself a wife?" Jodie asked lightly. "I know there's a shortage of women here in Alaska, but you're attractive and make a decent living. And you're good with children. There must be plenty of women who'd walk down the aisle with you."

Donovan set the mask back on the table with a grim expression. "I don't believe in marriage, that's why. Somebody usually ends up getting burned."

Jodie swallowed. Maybe she didn't need to know that much about him. So what if Donovan didn't think she was right for his brother? It was Cole's opinion that counted.

"My dad walked out on us when I was Tadd's age," Donovan continued. "He took all the money, leaving a woman with two small kids to manage alone in the dead of winter."

"I'm sorry," she whispered.

He let out a humorless laugh. "We survived. But from what I can tell, more marriages end in divorce than ever succeed. It isn't worth the effort and mess to clean up."

"Your mother doesn't feel that way."

"My mother is a romantic." Donovan crossed his arms over his chest. He hated talking about his childhood, but something about Jodie had unhinged his tongue—in more ways than one. "Mom got lucky the second time around, that's all. It could have gone either way."

Jodie put the beaded vest she'd been examining back on the table. She seemed to be searching for words. "But your partners—it sounds like they're happy with their wives and families."

He shrugged. "So far, so good, at least on the current go-around. Mike married a girl who's been in love with him her entire life. As for Ross...his first wife was a nightmare. She used their kid to get money from him after the divorce. He married Hannah three years ago, hoping a wife would help in case of a custody battle.''

"How lovely for Hannah," Jodie said dryly.

"It's okay. They think they're in love now."

A flash of anger crossed Jodie's face. "Oh…they *think* they're in love. They aren't really, they just think so. What makes you an expert on their relationship? Or do you think love isn't important?"

His eyebrows shot upward. ''That's an interesting comment. Aren't you the one planning a mail-order marriage? It seems like you're only marrying Cole to get away from your father's interference. There isn't much love in that kind of arrangement.''

Jodie flushed, looking angrier than ever. "My father has nothing to do with this. And I happen to believe in love, I just don't want my heart to get broken again. That's all.''

"How lovely for Cole."

Her breath hissed out, and for a moment Donovan thought he might get his face slapped. He shouldn't have used her own words against her; Ross and Hannah's situation was different than Jodie and Cole's. He didn't have any business comparing the two couples.

Damn his big mouth. He kept skating over the edge with Jodie. Truthfully he didn't know how to deal with someone like her. She had a curious mix of strength and fragility that confused him…a vulnerability that touched a chord deep inside his soul.

"Look, I'm sorry," Donovan murmured. He thrust his fingers in his pockets and smiled his most charming smile. "I shouldn't have said that. Chalk it up to a lack of sleep. I'm not thinking clearly."

"You sound pretty clear to me."

He paused, wishing he could understand the emotions churning in Jodie's green eyes. There was nothing superficial or casual about her, nothing he could dismiss. She certainly didn't fit into a comfortable category like the other women he'd dated.

Not that he was dating Jodie, Donovan quickly assured himself. They were spending time together because Cole wasn't here and his mother was determined to keep her in Alaska.

Except…it felt an awful lot like dating. Especially since he wanted to kiss Jodie again.

A real kiss.

A kiss she meant to give *him*, instead of one based on mistaken identity. A knot formed in Donovan's stomach, composed of equal parts of panic and anger at himself.

He cleared his throat. "This is strange for all of us, Jodie. And I have a gift for saying the wrong thing to you. Love is a touchy subject for me…I don't really believe in it."

"Because of your father?"

He thought back, testing the memories and finding them as bitter as they'd always been. "Dad said he loved Mom—loved all of us. He said it all the time, and he still walked out. Times were tough and he couldn't take it. Love sure didn't keep him there."

"So because *he* left, love isn't worth anything?" Jodie put her hand on his arm. Her eyes had darkened, becoming even harder to read. "It was a flaw in your father, that's all. Do you suppose a man like

Shamus would walk out on his family, no matter how difficult times were?''

Since Donovan had never considered Shamus a father, he'd never considered the idea. But when he tried to envision Shamus abandoning his family, it was difficult to imagine.

''I don't know,'' Donovan admitted slowly.

''Maybe you should think about it.''

Chapter Five

Two hours later Jodie was still biting her tongue. She didn't have any right to comment on Donovan's life or his family. She'd had her share of problems with General McBride, but they were mostly with him taking too much responsibility and trying to run her life.

What did she know about a parent's desertion? Or the scars it left on the children? Was it the same as losing a father through death?

A chill crept across her skin as Jodie looked at Tadd and Penny. Her son had been angry when his dad was killed, angry at God and life and airplanes. Even angry at Mark for dying. Would he grow up like Donovan, determined to keep love and marriage out of his future?

No. She rubbed her arms to warm them. The two situations were different. She could see why Donovan had grown up questioning the value of love after his father left. Maybe even questioning his self-worth. Nevertheless he still seemed to be a well-adjusted, easygoing guy with friends and a normal life.

"Jodie?"

She blinked and looked at the subject of her thoughts, standing nearby with Penny perched on his shoulders, enjoying an airy view of the arena.

"Yes?"

"Are you still upset about our—" he hesitated "—our discussion?"

"Not the way you think," she murmured, her brooding glance sweeping over Tadd and Penny again. She often wondered how children survived growing up, and how parents survived worrying about their kids. This was one of those times.

"Hey, it's okay for us to disagree—we're going to be in-laws," he kidded. "We're not supposed to get along."

"Your mother would object to that opinion," Jodie returned, a smile tugging at her mouth.

"Mom thinks you're terrific," Donovan said quietly.

Mom thinks you're terrific.

But her eldest son didn't, something becoming all too obvious to Jodie. It shouldn't matter, but it did. Even the things he'd said about marriage showed he was uncertain about her. And the things he'd said about her and Cole.

It seems like you're only marrying Cole to get away from your father's interference.

Did Donovan think she was so incapable of managing her life, that she needed a husband to protect them from General McBride? Another, even more unpleasant thought occurred to Jodie. Did Donovan think she needed a man to support her?

Jodie stirred restlessly. It was one thing to say Donovan Masters's opinion didn't matter, but another to be perceived as a weak-willed woman in need of a big, strong man to play Tarzan to her Jane.

"Mom, this is *so* great," Tadd exclaimed, unable to take his gaze off the blanket toss demonstration in front of them. It wasn't part of the competition, but an impromptu get-together among friends.

A group of men held a walrus hide blanket stretched out between them. Another man was in the middle of the blanket, being tossed high into the air. Up and down, miraculously remaining on his feet as he landed, reaching heights of twenty feet or more.

Penny clapped her hands and screamed with delight each time the man rose into the air. Donovan held her legs securely, somehow anticipating the erratic movements of an excited little girl.

A sweet, piercing ache went through Jodie at the sight. Penny was so certain Donovan was her new daddy. She accepted him fully, without reservation, confident he would hold and protect her.

Please, God, let her feel that way about Cole, too, Jodie prayed silently. Yet it wasn't Penny she worried most about, it was Tadd. He already looked at Donovan with a fair amount of hero worship and had been making not-so-subtle hints about whom his mother ought to marry.

The man being tossed on the blanket finally came down and lost his balance. His fellow participants laughed, good-natured ribbing having accompanied each end to a successful series of tosses.

"Want to have a go, Donovan?" called one of the men. "You were pretty good once."

"What do you mean, once?"

"That was before you grew into such a beanpole."

"Beanpole, huh? I can't let that go by without a challenge." Donovan laughed and shifted Penny from his shoulders to Shamus's. He cracked his fingers and flexed his legs several times. "Okay, George, put your money where your mouth is."

"Sure. If you stay upright for three landings, you and the family get a three-day fishing trip at the lodge. If you don't, you fly three tourists into the lake for free."

"Deal. But I expect some muscle in those tosses."

Donovan winked at Tadd as he crouched on the blanket. The last time he'd been tossed on a walrus hide he hadn't been much older than the boy, and he understood the envious expression on the youngster's face.

Six tosses later, George cheerfully conceded that Donovan could indeed still stay on his feet, despite his size. He hadn't risen as high as the more skilled participants, but he'd remained upright on the landings often enough to win the bet.

"Is that the deluxe fishing trip?" Donovan asked, clasping his hand on his friend's shoulder. "Food, tour guide, the whole routine?"

"You bet." George chuckled. "It'll be a real pleasure to have that woman of yours around for a few days. Funny, but I don't recall you gettin' married."

Donovan swallowed. "I didn't. Actually, she's sort of Cole's fiancée."

George looked Jodie up and down, taking in her long legs, slender waist and lush curves. He shook his head and whistled. "If I was you, I'd drop Cole into the nearest river, then make a move myself."

Donovan didn't need anyone pointing out Jodie's feminine appeal. She had the kind of looks that made a man do insane things, but disloyalty to his brother wasn't one of them.

"She's interested in getting a husband, and I'm not the marrying kind," he muttered.

"That's a real shame." George walked toward Tadd and made a broad gesture with his hand. "How about a toss, young man? You look like you've got springs in your knees."

Thrilled, Tadd spun to his mother. "Can I, Mom?"

"May I," Jodie corrected automatically.

"May I, pleeeeze."

"They'll be careful," Donovan assured her, seeing the concern in her green eyes. He could tell Jodie was overprotective, yet she fought her natural instincts to keep the children close and safe. Everything was on her shoulders. No shared responsibilities for a single mom, just a constant battle, trying to be both mother and father.

His own protective instincts hovered close to the surface, not for Tadd or Penny, but for the young woman who bit her lip, mentally gauging the safety of another unknown adventure. His own mother must have had similar moments of uncertainty, and he had a new appreciation of what she'd gone through all those years ago, alone with two young sons.

"Come on, Mom," Tadd pleaded.

"They won't toss him high, just enough to get the feel of it," Donovan said quietly. He understood Jodie's reluctance. Some of the events at the WEIO had resulted in injury that day. Strength and endurance were part of these unique Olympic games; they certainly weren't for the fainthearted.

"All…right," she agreed.

Tadd grabbed Donovan's hand and dragged him forward. "Show me how, Donovan."

From the side, Jodie watched her son eagerly listening to Donovan and the instructions from the other men. It would be easy to pretend they were a family, enjoying the day together. Several people had already made that mistake.

Evelyn had comfortably explained to her acquaintances that Jodie was a friend of her son Cole. She hadn't said they were engaged, probably for fear she'd jinx the thing.

Jinx?

A wry smile lifted Jodie's mouth. Wasn't it already jinxed? Between Cole's decision to climb McKinley and her growing attraction to Donovan, the whole thing seemed precarious at best. She'd never believed widows were insatiable and love-starved, but her body was reminding her that she was still alive and functioning.

Drat.

Jodie closed her eyes, trying to block Donovan from her sight. It didn't help, because she still saw him in her mind, jumping powerfully off the walrus hide blanket. His friend had called Donovan a beanpole, but there was nothing stringy or unfinished about him. He was very much a man, with the right complement of muscles and masculine grace.

"See me, Mom?"

She looked in time to see Tadd go a few feet up in the air. He urged the others to toss him higher and she tensed.

"Not your first time," Donovan said firmly. He stood near the men holding the blanket, his body posed for action if it was needed.

Jodie relaxed. Donovan might not approve of her, but he wouldn't let her son get hurt. She could trust him, at least that much. Their eyes met through the ring of tossers, and her breathing faltered.

"Tadd must be a fine athlete," Evelyn said, breaking the spell. "He's doing so well for a beginner."

Blinking, Jodie focused on Evelyn. "Yes, he's very active."

"Daddy, me go," called Penny from her perch on Shamus's shoulders. "I go fly."

"No," Jodie said instantly. If she'd worried about Tadd jumping on that blanket, it was ten times worse thinking of Penny flying through the air.

"Aw, Penny, you're too little," Tadd said. He'd finished his blanket-tossing lessons and looked utterly disgusted at the idea of his baby sister trying such a grown-up activity.

"Not little." Penny's face clouded and her bottom lip stuck out. "Me go, Mommy." Two fat tears rolled down her cheeks.

Donovan took one look at the crying child and his heart contracted. "We could swing her up and down without tossing her," he said.

"Yeah," chorused the men behind him. They looked equally distressed.

Four more tears dripped from Penny's green eyes and Donovan started feeling desperate. "I promise she won't ever lose contact with the blanket."

He heard a distinct sigh from Jodie. "Boy, are you gullible. All right, she can go."

"Come along, Penny. Mommy says you can have a swing on the blanket." Donovan held out his arms to the child and she launched herself at him with a giggle.

"Fly, Daddy."

Disconcerted by the lightning change from sorrow to smiles, he looked at Jodie. "What happened?"

"Crocodile tears," she said distinctly. "They work every time."

Instead of being annoyed, Donovan chuckled and hugged Penny closer. The feminine wiles that annoyed him in grown women were whimsical and charming in a two-year-old. He set her in the middle of the walrus hide blanket and the men grabbed the edges, lifting it, then cautiously swinging her up and down.

Penny's happy shrieks of laughter drew attention from the other visitors, and a number of people paused to watch. It was a long way from the traditional blanket toss, but indulging a child held a universal appeal.

"Who's ready for salmon and ribs?" asked Evelyn when Penny was finished and had climbed off the blanket.

"Me," Tadd said instantly.

Donovan laughed at the way Jodie rolled her eyes. He remembered that bottomless-pit sensation from boyhood—the need to consume everything in sight and then look for seconds.

"We're going to the salmon bake, then?" he asked Shamus.

"Evie thought it might fill the lad up for an hour or so."

"Just long enough to get him home," Donovan added, a droll note to his voice.

Shamus chuckled. "He's a good lad. The husky team took to him like green to grass. They know a right one, for certain."

Donovan looked at Jodie in time to see her flush with pleasure at the overheard comment. She was so proud of the kids. They might exasperate her at times, but overall there was a conspicuous love for Penny and Tadd that outweighed everything else.

For the first time in his life, Donovan wondered what it would be like to have children. *Really* wondered. Since he didn't want to get married, he'd never thought about having a family. Why think about kids when you'd never take the first step to have them?

But Jodie and her children...They made him think.

A man would be proud to claim Tadd and Penny. And deep inside, Donovan felt a low burning anger at the man who had recklessly ended his life before he ever saw his second child. If Mark Richards had been more careful, he would still be alive to take care of his family. Richards had lived dangerously, knowing he had responsibilities, but he'd left Jodie alone with a baby on the way and another son to raise. In some ways it wasn't that different from Donovan's own father.

"Is something wrong, lad?" Shamus asked, shattering his concentration.

Donovan shook himself and looked around. Jodie, his mother and the children were walking toward one of the exits. "I was just thinking."

Shamus waited, too tactful to ask, but plainly questioning what troubled his stepson.

"Jodie said her husband died because he was going too fast and taking unnecessary chances," Donovan muttered. "It was a damned selfish way to live."

"Aye."

There were a lot of things he wanted to say to Shamus, only he wasn't ready. He needed to think some more, particularly about what Jodie had suggested—about his stepfather not being the kind of man to abandon his family.

"Well—" Donovan forced a smile "—I guess it was tough, but Jodie made it. And she'll have help if she marries Cole."

Shamus nodded thoughtfully. "Though I doubt the lass needs it," he said. "Jodie has a bit of steel down her spine."

"It's just that Irish stubbornness."

The elder man's eyes twinkled. "Aye, lad. Irish stubbornness goes a long way."

Donovan took the last bite of his porterhouse steak and decided he'd eaten enough for a week. The salmon bake was too tempting, though he noticed Jodie had eaten far more lightly than everyone else—mostly salad from the salad bar.

"Don't you like salmon?" he asked softly, remembering she'd given most of her fish to Shamus.

She smiled. "Yes, but I'm not a lumberjack, and those are lumberjack portions."

He grinned and swiped a piece of sourdough roll around his plate, then popped it into his mouth. "You'll never grow into a big, tough Alaskan if you eat like a rabbit."

To Donovan's surprise, Jodie's smile faded.

"I've grown enough, thank you."

He allowed his gaze to skim her taut curves and slender waist. "I'll allow you grew in the right places," he said, trying to regain a lighter note.

Nothing had been entirely comfortable though, not since their so-called discussion at the arena. Donovan tried to remember exactly what had been said, and when Jodie had withdrawn into herself. As he recalled, it was somewhere between deadbeat fathers and the questionable values of love. Then there was that stupid comment he'd made about Cole, which couldn't have earned him many points in the diplomacy department.

Considering his loose tongue, it might be wise to avoid spending time with Jodie.

"Son," Evelyn said, looking down the table, "would you run by Cole's house on the way home and get my large coffeepot? I'll need it when Ross and Mike get here."

"Sounds good. I imagine Jodie would like to see the place," Donovan suggested without thinking.

"No...that is, maybe later." If Evelyn had looked alarmed earlier at the thought of Jodie staying at a motel, she appeared downright panicked at the idea of Jodie seeing her youngest son's home.

Belatedly Donovan remembered his brother

wasn't the best housekeeper in the world. Really, he was getting himself in deeper all the time.

"That's a good idea," Jodie said, obviously missing her hostess's consternation.

"Well, Cole left in such a hurry, I'm sure it's a little…messy," Evelyn stuttered. "You should probably wait until he gets home before going over."

Jodie shrugged. "Don't worry. I can take some mess. And Cole was concerned it wouldn't be big enough for the four of us, so I should get an idea about how much space he has."

Briefly Donovan wondered if there was any danger of the health department declaring Cole's house a health hazard. It might scare Jodie off completely, but she had a right to know that her so-called fiancé lacked basic domestic instincts.

"Okay, we'll go on the way home. But Mom and Shamus should take the kids," Donovan added hastily. He didn't want Penny frightened by the nine-foot-tall stuffed grizzly bear Cole had gotten several years ago from one of his clients.

"All right." Jodie deftly held Penny's wrists, holding her sticky fingers away from both of them. "I'll clean her up, then we can switch the child's seat into your folks' car."

"Okay."

He watched her leave with Penny and groaned silently. He'd just decided he shouldn't spend so much time with Jodie, then he'd invited her on a private outing with him. His mouth should be declared a disaster area.

"Donovan…" Evelyn said sternly. "How could

you suggest going to Cole's? Jodie will have heart failure."

"She should see him at his worst. Besides, maybe Cole cleaned the place before he found out about the climb." They were brave words, but Donovan's voice lacked conviction. He didn't really believe it.

"In a pig's eye." Apparently his mother didn't believe it, either.

"Here we go," Donovan said, flinging the door open and motioning Jodie to precede him.

She walked in and her eyes widened. Based on Evelyn's consternation about her seeing Cole's house, she'd expected it to be disorganized. But the sight was still a shock. She was accustomed to military neatness, not...*this*.

No wonder Evelyn Carney had nearly swooned. It was a certified disaster area.

Still waiting by the door, Donovan cleared his throat. "I guess things got away from Cole. I'm sure he meant to...er, straighten up before you got to Alaska."

Jodie turned and couldn't suppress a startled scream. Somehow she'd missed seeing the stuffed bear standing to the left of the entry. It loomed over the wreckage as though afraid to drop down on all fours in case it got lost in the sea of clothing, newspapers, pizza boxes and sporting equipment.

"Sorry about that," Donovan muttered.

"That's okay." A giggle quickly followed Jodie's initial shriek.

"The bear is...I was afraid it would scare Penny," Donovan stuttered.

Jodie looked it up and down. "It might be alarming."

The poor thing was being used as a coat rack, which diminished its menacing appearance. Snowshoes hung from one of its outstretched arms, along with a down jacket, knitted ski cap and athletic supporter.

Donovan saw the athletic supporter and groaned. He snatched the offending article from its perch and stuffed it in his pocket. For the hundredth time in the past two days he wanted to strangle his little brother. Couldn't Cole have gotten rid of the bear *before* Jodie arrived? And why hadn't he transformed this wasteland into something a woman would be reassured at seeing?

It wasn't a bad house—three bedrooms, a family room, two and a half baths, and a cathedral ceiling in the living room. Donovan didn't give a hoot about the ceiling, but Cole had been pleased since it meant the nine-foot "Harvey" could stand at full attention.

"I'll go look for the coffeepot," Jodie murmured. Her tone suggested she might have trouble locating it and to send out a search party if she went missing for very long.

"I'm really sorry," he apologized again, but Jodie just shook her head and laughed. "At least I know I'm needed," she said, sounding both amused and resigned.

Donovan stared at the wreckage and wondered how he could be so different from a brother just five years younger than him. He didn't claim to be a neat freak, but he wasn't a slob, either.

The sound of clinking dishes and clanking pans drew his attention and he poked his head around the corner. Jodie had rolled up her sleeves and was filling the dishwasher. Her movements were swift and efficient, and for some reason the whole process irritated Donovan.

"You don't have to do that," he said sharply. "You're not married to him yet." Donovan paused. "That is…you shouldn't have to bother with his mess."

Jodie's eyes narrowed, then she motioned around the disorganized room. "I know, but I can't find the carafe or the plastic piece that holds the filter for the coffeemaker. I figured it would be easier to find all the pieces if it was cleaner in here."

Looking around the kitchen and dining area, Donovan silently agreed.

"I'll check upstairs," he said, not wanting to examine his flash of annoyance over Jodie slipping so quickly into the role of Cole's wife.

To Donovan's surprise, the second story was remarkably neat and tidy. Cole had apparently started the cleaning process, herding the mess down the stairs so he could deal with it in one place. At least that explained the revolting layers of bachelordom adorning the living room.

The only sign of disorder was in the room Cole used as a home office. His desk was scattered with wadded pieces of paper that spilled onto the floor and circled the waste can. Donovan automatically began gathering them together, then froze when he saw Jodie's name on one of the scrawled sheets.

"David, do you think Jodie would be upset if we waited a while before…"

The last words were scratched out.

Feeling guilty for prying, Donovan sat and flat-

tened a number of the crumpled sheets. They were
partly finished letters, some to Jodie, some to her
brother David. And in each of them, Cole was looking for a way out of the marriage he'd proposed. He
seemed worried both about his friendship with David, and about the half promises he'd made to Jodie.

"So, Cole *did* change his mind," Donovan muttered angrily.

Or maybe he hadn't. Cole had said he still intended on going through with the marriage when
he'd called and explained about the McKinley
climbing expedition.

Tell Jodie I still want to get married.

Perhaps it was Donovan's imagination, but when
he remembered his brother's voice, there was a
shade of hesitation in the words…a hint of reluctance to go through with the commitment he'd made
to Jodie and her children.

"Blasted, irresponsible idiot."

Donovan finished straightening the discarded letters and read them over and over, searching for an
answer. In the end, he was certain Cole had wanted
to call the wedding off, or to suggest they wait for
a while. But for some reason he hadn't found the
words, or mailed the letters to either Jodie or his
friend David.

What a lousy mess. Donovan leaned back in the
desk chair and scowled at the wall. He understood
Cole changing his mind about getting married, but
he didn't understand treating a woman so badly. For
two days he'd obsessed about honor and not feeling
desire for his brother's fiancée, when all along Cole
had run out on the situation.

And almost as bad, it looked as if Cole had left
his big brother to clean things up for him.

Chapter Six

Jodie kicked an errant soccer ball clear across the living room and watched it bounce off the wall.

She was really getting annoyed with Donovan.

"'You're not married to him *yet*,'" she mimicked under her breath. "'You'll never grow into a big, tough Alaskan if you eat like a rabbit.' Rabbit. Ha!"

Opening a plastic garbage bag, she began stuffing it with trash from the living room. She stomped on pizza boxes, crushed fast-food drink cups and smashed hamburger wrappers and newspapers into the bag. When it was full, she took another and filled it, as well. After the third bag, the room looked like a different place altogether.

No sounds came from the second floor, and Jodie couldn't decide if it annoyed her even more, or just capped the head of steam she was building.

It seems like you're only marrying Cole to get away from your father's interference.

No matter how hard she tried to forget it, that

statement kept repeating in her head like a broken record. "My father is none of his concern," she growled at the stuffed bear by the entry.

His beady eyes appeared to glint sympathetically, and she patted his shaggy forearm.

"Never mind, it's not your problem." The words weren't really for the bear, but for herself. She wanted to believe Donovan's opinion didn't matter.

Unfortunately it mattered too much.

With short, jerky movements, Jodie vacuumed the carpet. The family room and bathroom were already clean, so it didn't take long to decide the downstairs was passable. That left the second floor where Donovan had disappeared.

Jodie put Evelyn's coffeemaker by the front door, then stood at the bottom of the stairs and glared. Who did he think he was? Donovan Masters didn't have any business approving, or not approving of her.

Keep your mouth shut.

It was excellent advice, but she wasn't in the mood to heed good advice.

Dusting her hands on her jeans, Jodie started up the staircase. The first door was to a bedroom—very masculine and tidy. The bed was even made. The second door stood open, and inside she saw Donovan sitting at a desk, looking at a handful of papers.

"We can go now. I found all the pieces," she said abruptly. "Of the coffeemaker."

"What?" Donovan jumped as though he'd been shot, and he slapped the papers facedown on the desk. "Jodie."

She waited, but he didn't say anything else and her temper had reached the boiling point.

"Yes, *Jodie.* I want to know what you meant before, about me 'not being married to Cole yet.' It was awfully strange the way you said that. Or that stuff about marrying him just to get away from my father."

Donovan looked at Jodie and groaned. Light from the window framed her, slanting across her breasts and turning her hair into a halo of rumpled gold. But there was nothing angelic about the way she was steaming.

"You don't think I should marry Cole, do you?" she demanded. "For some reason you don't approve of me. That's it, isn't it?"

Donovan put a paperweight on the letters he'd been reading and laid his hands flat on the surface of the desk. "It isn't you, Jodie."

"Sure. I believe that."

"It's complicated."

"Complicated, my foot. There are at least three strikes against me." Jodie lifted her hand and counted off on her fingers. "I don't wear the right clothing. I don't like Cole's mountain climbing. And I wasn't born and bred in your precious Alaska. Actually, change that to four reasons—I'm a woman."

Donovan breathed slowly, determined this once to watch what he said. "Can we forget about the clothing? I was out of line when I said that—it was inexcusable."

"Yes," she said flatly.

"And I don't hate women, I just don't believe in marriage...for myself," Donovan added.

"Or for Cole." There was genuine hurt and bewilderment in Jodie's eyes. "I'm sorry you don't think I'm right for your brother, but this isn't your decision."

Guilt churned in Donovan's stomach, both for the way he'd acted toward Jodie since she'd arrived in Alaska, and the knowledge that Cole probably *had* made his decision. Lord, it was complicated. But then, Jodie wasn't an uncomplicated sort of woman.

Donovan sighed. At the moment, he needed to get her far away from those damning, half-written letters. But most of all, he needed to shake his little brother until his teeth rattled.

If Cole hadn't started writing Jodie in the first place, then she wouldn't have arrived in Alaska, only to be met by a stranger. She wouldn't have mistakenly kissed the wrong man at the airport. And they wouldn't be having this discussion.

It was all Cole's fault…except the part Donovan had left out. The part where he'd been rude to Jodie. The part where he wanted to kiss her senseless, even believing she might be marrying his brother. And the part where he'd lost his mind. That pretty much covered everything.

"Well?" Jodie said, the hurt in her eyes dissolving into anger.

"I don't think you're wrong for Cole, I'm just…" Donovan paused, unable to keep from glancing at the crumpled papers on the desk. "I'm not sure he's ready for marriage."

"That isn't your call."

Jumping to his feet, Donovan went around the desk, deliberately blocking Jodie's view. He didn't want her getting curious to see what he'd been reading.

"And you *don't* approve of me," she repeated.

"I'm not some helpless woman, needing a husband to take care of me and the children. We can manage just fine on our own."

He rubbed his temples wearily. "I never said you couldn't."

"You said I was marrying Cole to get away from my father," she accused. "I'm not a rebellious teenager anymore. I don't have to marry a man to get out of the house."

"Uh-huh," he said, not really listening. He was too busy calculating the best way to get Jodie away from the incriminating evidence in Cole's office. "We should go home now. It's getting late."

"*Donovan.* I want to know what it is you don't like about me."

She plainly wasn't going anywhere until she'd gotten the answers she wanted. Well, he could understand that. He'd pushed her for answers more than once since she'd arrived.

"Uh…your father," he murmured. "I can understand why it's important for you to get some distance from him. He must be difficult to live with."

Jodie rolled her eyes. "I would have moved more than a year ago, but he'd just been diagnosed with diabetes and the doctors were trying to stabilize his condition. I wanted to stay and help. You can understand that, right?"

Nodding, Donovan sat on the corner of the desk and watched Jodie. The poised, cool woman who'd gotten off the plane was gone. In her place was a temptress—cheeks flushed, temper flaring and passion simmering like an emerald fire.

A matching heat burned low in his groin.

If Cole saw Jodie like this, he'd throw caution to the wind and marry her despite his doubts.

"I'm financially independent," Jodie said, a shade more calmly. "There's plenty of money between Mark's life insurance and the survivor's annuity. I needed my father in the beginning because of Penny, but that was only temporary."

Donovan didn't know what to say. His preconceptions were wrong, as usual, and he didn't have a defense. If he'd used his head, he would have realized Jodie was too stubborn to stay in Florida if she didn't want to.

"For that matter," she declared, "I could go back to work. I have a degree in business management. Before we moved to Turkey I managed the base officers' club. They said I could come back anytime."

"I never said—"

"Do you want a background check on me? To make sure I'm not some raving lunatic? Is that it?" Jodie demanded. "My father did one on Cole, and you're welcome to check me out, as well. I don't have anything to hide, so investigate away."

That caught Donovan's attention and his gaze narrowed. "General McBride did a background check on my family?"

"Yeah. He's very thorough—he hired a private investigator, then ran Cole through every official government computer in existence. He was hoping for some delicious family skeletons to rattle in front of me."

"Then you already knew about my dad leaving us," Donovan muttered, feeling exposed in a way he'd never felt before.

Here's a **HOT** offer for you!

Get set for a sizzling summer read...

with **2 FREE ROMANCE BOOKS** and a **FREE MYSTERY GIFT!**

NO CATCH! NO OBLIGATION TO BUY!

Simply complete and return this card and you'll get **2 FREE BOOKS** and **A FREE GIFT** – yours to keep!

Visit us online at www.eHarlequin.com

- The first shipment is yours to keep, **absolutely free!**
- Enjoy the convenience of Silhouette Romance® books delivered right to your door, before they're available in stores!
- Take advantage of special low pricing for **Reader Service Members only!**
- After receiving your free books we hope you'll want to remain a subscriber. But the choice is always yours—to continue or cancel, any time at all! So why not take us up on this fabulous invitation, with no risk of any kind. You'll be glad you did!

315 SDL C4FD

215 SDL C4FC

(S-R-OS-07/00)

▼ DETACH HERE AND MAIL CARD TODAY! ▶

Name: _____
(Please Print)

Address: _____ Apt.#: _____

City: _____

State/Prov.: _____ Zip/Postal Code: _____

Offer limited to one per household and not valid to current Silhouette Romance® subscribers. All orders subject to approval. © 1998 HARLEQUIN ENTERPRISES LTD. ® & TM are trademarks owned by Harlequin Books S.A. used under license.

The Silhouette Reader Service™ —Here's how it works:

Accepting your 2 free books and gift places you under no obligation to buy anything. You may keep the books and gift and return the shipping statement marked "cancel." If you do not cancel, about a month later we'll send you 6 additional novels and bill you just $2.90 each in the U.S., or $3.25 each in Canada, plus 25¢ delivery per book and applicable taxes if any.* That's the complete price and — compared to cover prices of $3.50 each in the U.S. and $3.99 each in Canada — it's quite a bargain! You may cancel at any time, but if you choose to continue, every month we'll send you 6 more books, which you may either purchase at the discount price or return to us and cancel your subscription.

*Terms and prices subject to change without notice. Sales tax applicable in N.Y. Canadian residents will be charged applicable provincial taxes and GST.

If offer card is missing write to: Silhouette Reader Service, 3010 Walden Ave., P.O. Box 1867, Buffalo, NY 14240-1867

BUSINESS REPLY MAIL
FIRST-CLASS MAIL   PERMIT NO. 717   BUFFALO, NY

POSTAGE WILL BE PAID BY ADDRESSEE

SILHOUETTE READER SERVICE
3010 WALDEN AVE
PO BOX 1867
BUFFALO NY 14240-9952

NO POSTAGE
NECESSARY
IF MAILED
IN THE
UNITED STATES

A background check?

Jeez.

She must know every detail about his mother having to work two jobs, the hand-me-down clothing and the times they didn't have enough to eat. Donovan wasn't ashamed of those times, but it flicked a raw spot nonetheless. Only, it wasn't so much his penniless childhood, but the way his own father had treated them, and how some private investigator would describe it.

After all these years, after building a successful business, there was still a part of Donovan that wondered why they hadn't been good enough for his dad to stay…if *he* hadn't been good enough.

"The good general must have had a field day with that report," Donovan said tightly, his jaw clenched. "I hope it spelled everything out, including the time Cole and I stole a decent coat for Mother to wear. We were dirt-poor, you see. She wouldn't spend money on herself and we couldn't stand seeing her go without."

"I never read the report," Jodie whispered, seeing the pain in Donovan's face. She hadn't meant to raise unpleasant memories, just to understand.

She liked Donovan—some of the time. She liked his family and their openhearted acceptance of her children. She hated the feeling she didn't measure up in his eyes. And most of all, she didn't like knowing how important Donovan's opinion had become in such a short time.

"Why not?"

"Because it didn't matter. Cole is David's friend, and David is a good judge of character," Jodie said quietly. "And I could tell a lot from the letters Cole wrote."

"Yeah, the letters." Something flickered in Donovan's eyes, but she couldn't tell what it meant, or if it meant anything at all.

She shivered and rubbed her arms. So far, she had nothing but Donovan's vague assurances that he thought she was "okay." No real explanations about his seemingly critical comments, or the odd way he had of looking at her.

"For what it's worth," Jodie said, "my father was frustrated because he couldn't find anything in the report to stop me from coming. He wasn't thrilled to admit it, but he said you all measured up. Not that you had to measure up, or that it was his place to make that judgment," she added quickly.

"But he still didn't want you to come."

Jodie shrugged. "He wants me to marry an officer on the fast track to the Pentagon. Someone likely to become a member of the Joint Chiefs of Staff, or some other nonsense."

"Sets his sights low, does he?"

Her low chuckle resonated through Donovan, reminding him of the desire riding him. Jodie Richards was too damned tempting. He'd never had so much trouble controlling his body around a woman...at least not since he was a teenager.

That was how she made him feel, like a teenager with feet too big and a tongue tied in knots. Jodie had grown up all over the world, experiencing things he'd only imagined. What could she have in common with a bush pilot from Alaska? And it was even more alarming to find himself thinking in those terms.

Alarming to find himself wondering about their differences, and how important they really were.

It wasn't the way to stay single, and he had every intention of staying single. He figured it wasn't in his nature to get married.

"Mom will be worried," Donovan said, a gruff note in his voice. "We should go."

"You still haven't answered me."

He thought about it. There'd been plenty of accusations flying, and he'd done the best to answer them without saying or doing something he shouldn't. Some things he couldn't answer without admitting his own attraction to Jodie…which didn't seem wise under the circumstances.

"Uh…about what?" he asked. "I don't disapprove of you. How could I? We barely know each other. And you're right, Cole is the one to decide if he's ready for a wife and family. That about covers it."

"What did you mean downstairs? When you came in and I was doing the dishes?" Jodie said stubbornly. "You thought I was being presumptuous. Stepping out of my proper place—I'm not a real fiancée yet, so I shouldn't get carried away with myself. Isn't that right?"

Donovan winced, remembering his irritation at finding Jodie cleaning Cole's kitchen. That was the problem with mixed signals. He'd thought and felt one thing, and she'd heard something else altogether.

Well, hell. Maybe clearing the air was the best thing after all.

He rocked forward on the balls of his feet, vaguely aware he was close to doing something he'd

regret. "Presumptuous? Not a chance. I admire anyone's courage in attacking that disaster. What I
didn't like…what *still* puts my tail in a knot, is seeing you jump right into the housewife routine."

Because I'm jealous of my brother, even if I don't
want to be.

Jodie made an impatient gesture. "I don't see the
difference."

A low, growling noise came from Donovan's
throat. "You, Jodie. Seeing *you* in Cole's kitchen."

"Right." She threw up her hands, sparks flying
again from her eyes. "Me. Because I don't belong
in Alaska or married to your brother."

He wasn't making himself clear. The woman
short-circuited the currents in his brain, making his
normally comfortable perspective on life go completely haywire.

She lifted her chin. "Thank you for clarifying
the—"

"*Damn.*" With a single expletive, Donovan's
arms shot out and he grabbed Jodie. Shock made the
words freeze in her mouth and she stared at him.

"Donovan?"

"I want you. I can't look at you without imagining what it would feel like to have you under me.
Then you go act like Cole's wife, and you haven't
even met him. Do you expect me to enjoy it?"

She took a shaky breath. "But you don't…"

"Want to get married," he finished for her. "I
have no intention of ever getting married. And I sure
as hell won't make love to a woman with wedding
rings in her eyes," he snapped.

"You arrogant, impossible…*moron.*" She stuttered to a halt, her repertoire of insults limited to

military allusions that wouldn't mean anything to him. "I never said I'd make love with you!"

"I never said you would. I just meant...oh, *hell.*"

Jodie's heart pumped furiously as he pulled her flush with his body. His fingers were splayed across her rib cage, just below her breasts, and she was suddenly, sensuously aware of their weight.

It had been so long since she'd felt this rush of adrenaline, not since she was girl, falling in love for the first time. The thought alone threatened to splash water on her excitement, but Donovan wasn't giving her time to breathe, much less rationalize the reasons she shouldn't be alone with him.

"Just making everything clear. Wouldn't want you to keep misunderstanding me," he muttered before bending to reach her mouth.

Instinctively her lips parted, accepting the kiss. It was gentle, undemanding at first, as though he was waiting to see if she'd object.

But Jodie couldn't resist. Deep in her heart, she knew she'd wanted Donovan to kiss her again. A second kiss, to see if she'd been wrong about her reaction to him at the airport. She swayed slightly, angling her neck to give him better access.

Then all at once his hand slid over her bottom, lifting her higher, while his other arm wrapped hard about her waist. The speed and fierceness stunned Jodie, though her body responded with the same intense need. Donovan might look easygoing and relaxed, but there were some things he didn't handle so calmly.

A second later her feet left the ground and the kiss turned into a steamy mating of open mouths.

Mmm. The rough velvet of his tongue thrust between her teeth. He tasted of coffee and the blueberry cake that had finished their meal, and every coherent thought fled her mind except the need to get closer.

Twisting to free her arms, Jodie slid them about his waist, filling her senses with his masculine scent and feel. She wanted to touch his bare skin, and she pulled at the tails of his shirt with an urgency that would have shocked her if she'd been able to think.

This is insane.

Donovan groaned and tried to regain control, but it seemed impossible with Jodie's fingers eagerly exploring his back. He'd started this—it was his responsibility to end it. But he hadn't expected such a passionate response. In the back of his head he remembered speculating about a fire burning beneath Jodie's elegant exterior, yet he couldn't have imagined this kind of passion, not in his wildest dreams.

He sank to his knees on the carpet, bringing her with him, and a moment later he was stretched out at her side, trailing a series of kisses down her jaw and pressing more into the hollow of her throat.

The faint scent of perfume infused his senses and he felt drunk on the sensual fragrance.

"Jodie..." he breathed, lightly stroking the tips of her breasts. They peaked instantly, the nipples pressing against the soft fabric of her blouse.

Donovan yanked his hand away as though it had been burned. It was insane to take this any further; he couldn't take the chance of discovering how responsive Jodie actually was, or how much he really wanted her.

With another groan, Donovan rolled aside and

threw his arm over his face. He dragged deep, harsh breaths into his lungs, desperately trying to get enough oxygen to think with his head, rather than his body.

He shouldn't have started anything. But he had. From almost the beginning of the argument he'd known he would kiss Jodie, and the knowledge burned in his conscience like a corrosive acid.

"I'm sorry," he muttered.

Jodie stared at the ceiling, still trembling from the aftermath of Donovan's kiss. She put her fingers to her lips, convinced they were singed. She'd never felt anything like that. It had been fast, explosive and darned near cataclysmic.

Of course, other than that, it wasn't anything remarkable.

She swallowed a hysterical giggle and tried to pull herself together. It was ridiculous letting a man affect her so much. She'd been in love, gotten married and then lost it all. Now she wanted something else, something less perilous to her peace of mind.

From the corner of her eye Jodie watched Donovan and realized he'd wasn't just perilous, he was the worst thing that could happen to her.

If she was going to fall in love, it wouldn't be with a man who flew planes for a living. Or a man so adamantly against marriage. She'd choose someone who shared some of her interests. Someone who didn't have a dangerous career or turn her inside out with a single glance.

Someone safe.

Donovan Masters wasn't safe. He wasn't even housebroken.

He lay there, his chest still heaving and an arm

flung over his face. Every inch of him was pure, impressive male. She didn't even have to lift her head to see the evidence of his arousal.

Actually, that part of him wasn't just impressive, it was awesome.

Jodie moaned and closed her eyes, but it didn't help. The image was burned into her brain, just as the sensation of his strength and hardness pressed against her stomach was seared into her body.

She'd never been like this, even when she *was* married. Not that she hadn't enjoyed sex. Sex was one of the most pleasant aspects of marriage, though she'd always suspected men got more out of it than women. Now she wasn't so sure.

"That—" Jodie cleared her throat "—that can't happen again." She wanted to believe she sounded normal, but it wasn't true. Her voice was hoarse and low, like she hadn't used it in days.

"It was my fault. And you don't need to worry, I *won't* let it happen again."

Jodie frowned. While it was partly Donovan's doing, she didn't feel blameless in the situation. She was aware of him. She'd been aware of him from the first moment, before they'd ever spoken. He must have sensed it.

"Don't beat yourself up," she whispered. "I kissed you first."

"No you didn't." He sounded annoyed. "I'm the one who grabbed you. I'm the one who kissed first."

"I meant at the airport."

"Oh."

She focused on a dusty spider web in the corner of the ceiling. Cole apparently didn't look up when he was cleaning, or else he'd never kissed a woman while lying on the floor.

Lord, *Cole*.

How could she marry Cole after kissing his brother so…enthusiastically? This time it wasn't a case of mistaken identity. She could have stopped Donovan, but she hadn't.

"The airport doesn't count," he muttered. "You thought I was Cole."

Jodie lifted herself on one elbow and looked at Donovan. She would have gotten to her feet, but she didn't think her legs were ready to support her. "So you're taking responsibility for *that* kiss, too?"

"Well, I…" He shrugged. "I should have introduced myself quicker. I just didn't expect you to kiss me—er—kiss Cole. That is, I didn't think you'd—"

"Kiss a total stranger, right? A decent woman wouldn't do such a thing, right?"

"Don't bring that up again," Donovan snapped.

"What?"

"You know what I mean." Donovan knew he was drifting back into dangerous territory. Jodie still thought he didn't approve of her, but this had nothing to do with approving, or not approving of her. He liked Jodie; she aroused his body like no other woman, and she made him think things no self-respecting, dedicated bachelor would ever think.

There.

That was the problem in a nutshell. And now that Cole might be out of the picture, Donovan was stuck with that problem and he damn well didn't want to be. It was much easier just to feel guilty for lusting after his brother's fiancée.

Still, it didn't mean he couldn't use Cole as a defense.

"What about Cole?" Donovan asked. "We both owe him something."

"Men," Jodie muttered darkly. "You may owe Cole your loyalty, but I don't."

"How do you see that?"

"He went climbing on Mount McKinley, when we were supposed to be deciding if we want to get married. I don't owe him a thing."

"I told you—"

"It was the chance of a lifetime. Yes, you told me." Jodie took several breaths. "That's all good and fine, but if the shoe was on the other foot, he wouldn't feel any obligation to me, would he?"

She looked pointedly at Donovan. He seemed to be having trouble dealing with the subject, but she didn't care.

"You don't feel the slightest bit guilty kissing me?" he asked, ignoring her question.

"Nope."

At least not much, Jodie added silently.

She felt worse about letting her hormones go raging out of control. For getting close to a man her heart recognized as dangerous. The last thing she wanted was to be vulnerable to a man like Donovan, who tugged at a secret, inner part of herself she didn't want to risk again.

"But you don't need to worry," Jodie muttered. "I'm not interested in a repeat."

"Why the hell not?" Donovan demanded, his pride stung by her obvious rejection. She didn't feel guilty because of Cole, so why wouldn't she want to kiss him?

"We're incompatible," she explained.

"I thought we were pretty compatible."

Her eyebrows shot upward. "I don't mean in bed, though we'll never know for sure about *that*. What I meant is, we want different things."

"That's right. I want a good time in the sack. No commitments," Donovan said flatly. "While you want to get married. Thank God we have that straightened out."

Jodie held on to her temper with an effort. "Yes. My children need a father, and I want to have another baby. I've been honest with Cole—he knows exactly what I'm looking for. He thought it was fine."

Donovan didn't say anything and she squirmed defensively.

"I have a lot to offer Cole. I wouldn't be the only one benefiting from the arrangement."

"I'm sure of that."

Donovan looked her up and down. Jodie trembled, aware he was giving her a full, masculine appraisal. His gaze lingered frankly on her breasts, then her waist, and the apex of her thighs where she still ached from unrelieved desire. Her body reacted from the impact of that heated examination—nipples hardening into tight points, and warmth welling from deep in her abdomen.

"D-Donovan?"

"Actually, I think Cole would be getting the better part of the bargain," he said in a low rough tone. "The thought of taking you to bed every night certainly appeals to me."

Chapter Seven

The thought of taking you to bed every night certainly appeals to me.

Jodie bit her lip, trying to concentrate on the scenery going by outside the Jeep. She wanted to think of *anything* but Donovan's provocative statement. She ought to be annoyed with such a sexist statement, but it was hard to be angry with that kind of sensuous approval.

After what seemed like an eternity, Donovan pulled to a stop by the Carneys' house and flexed his fingers on the steering wheel. He didn't make a move to get out, and Jodie was equally uncertain what to do.

It seemed as though more should be said, but what?

There wasn't any manual on etiquette for mail-order marriages. And even if there was, how many women found themselves attracted to the brother of their groom-to-be?

"I guess we're agreed we should spend as little time together as possible," Jodie murmured finally.

"We're agreed."

She sneaked a look at Donovan's profile, wondering if he felt as grim as he sounded. "Okay."

All at once he turned toward her, an angry expression on his face. "Out of purely egotistical curiosity, why are you so certain we're incompatible? It's more than our difference of opinion about marriage, isn't it?"

Jodie swallowed. She couldn't explain without admitting that he disturbed her too much, that he was too much like a man she *could* love. If she'd met him as a girl, before falling in love with Mark Richards and being widowed, she would have chased after Donovan Masters with all the intensity a fearless teenager could muster.

But not now.

Now she knew what it was like to fall in love, only to get her heart smashed into tiny little pieces.

Still, she stole another glance at Donovan's tense face and searched for words that would satisfy him without revealing the truth. She didn't want him misunderstanding things, the way *she'd* misunderstood. If their signals hadn't gotten crossed, they wouldn't have kissed and nearly made love. If they slipped again it might be a disaster.

"Well?" he demanded.

"To be honest, you're too much like my first husband."

"I'm *what?*" Donovan looked at Jodie, astonished. It was the last thing he'd expected to hear. Sure, he knew he was a pilot, too, but that was only superficial. "You can't be serious."

She pushed her hair back with her fingers and shrugged. "There are some similarities."

Donovan was certain there was more to Jodie's explanation, and he suddenly knew that he didn't need to hear it. He already knew too much.

He knew Jodie smelled like an angel and kissed like a goddess. He knew her body was soft and sweetly rounded, and so responsive, he wouldn't be able to sleep remembering it.

Hell, for that matter he might never sleep again.

A woman had never turned him on quicker and harder. Donovan wanted to believe it was because she was unattainable. *Safe.* If they'd met under any other circumstances he would have promptly hightailed it away, because she was the permanent sort of woman he'd always avoided.

Only, Donovan couldn't deny he would have been too curious about Jodie to stay away. Unavailable or not, she'd become a fire in his blood that he couldn't seem to control.

"Well, it's getting late. And I'm tired." Jodie fumbled for the door handle, but was startled by Donovan's fingers closing around her wrist.

"Wait." Without another word he got out of the Jeep and walked around to her door. He opened it and he held out his hand.

Jodie swallowed. It wasn't a good idea touching Donovan. Her skin was still too sensitized to pretend he didn't affect her, and she'd never been good at pretending.

"Jodie?" he murmured when she didn't move. "Believe it or not, I *can* be a gentleman. My mother would be horrified if she knew how I've acted."

"About what part? Being rude or kissing me?"

Jodie asked, then groaned. "Uh…forget I said that."

His smile flashed. "It's already forgotten—I owe you a free one."

Still wary, Jodie put her hand in Donovan's, accepting his assistance from the high seat of the Jeep. She wasn't sure why he'd believed her earlier explanation. In reality, his few similarities to her first husband were rapidly fading from her mind.

Mark had never worried about anything. He'd just charged ahead, having too much fun to worry about "paying the piper" as he'd called it. A hothead, with too much ability and not enough discipline to control it.

But not Donovan. He wasn't devil-may-care, though he sometimes appeared that way. He showed concern for her children. He was thoughtful and seemed aware of the consequences of his actions. His father's desertion had touched him deeply, affecting his outlook on life. And while she didn't know what kind of pilot he was, Evelyn had proudly talked about the Triple M Transit's excellent safety record.

"You're welcome to fix some warm milk. It might help you sleep," Donovan said quietly once they'd gone inside in the house. Everything was quiet, suggesting the Carneys, along with Tadd and Penny, were in bed.

Jodie shook her head. She didn't want to spend another minute alone with Donovan. It was too disturbing. "No, I'll be fine."

She escaped quickly. The children were soundly asleep and she sank onto her own bed with a sigh of relief. Facing anyone after that scene in Cole's home office would have been more than she could handle.

"God," she moaned, covering her face with her hands. Her trip to Alaska was turning into the kind of nightmare even her father couldn't have predicted.

Flopping backward on the mattress, Jodie listened to the pad of Donovan's footsteps down the hall. She could hear Penny's soft breathing in the corner, curled cozily in a small child's bed.

Tadd and Penny. She hadn't been thinking of her children when she'd kissed Donovan. She hadn't been thinking at all.

Disgusted, Jodie turned on her side and gazed at the heavy curtains covering the windows. They dimmed the room, making it easier to sleep during an Alaska summer, when there was little or no darkness during the night.

No matter what, she was moving to Alaska. Fairbanks, if things worked out with her mail-order husband. Anchorage, if she didn't marry Cole. Otherwise, it would be awkward being so close to the Carneys.

Of course, if she moved to Anchorage, Donovan might think she was interested in him. He might even worry she was planning to go after him to get a wedding ring on her finger.

Donovan again.

"Urghhh!" Jodie shrieked, a pillow stuffed over her face to muffle the sound.

The man was becoming impossible to escape, even in her mind. If she had any sense, she'd pack up and leave before anything else happened.

Such as her heart getting broken.

* * *

Though Jodie had worried what to say to Donovan the next day, it wasn't a problem. Before anyone had gotten out of bed, he'd left for the Triple M Transit office. His note explained he had some work to do.

The news should have relieved Jodie; instead she felt perversely disappointed.

Evelyn outlined another day of sight-seeing, involving a riverboat cruise she thought Tadd would particularly enjoy. If she was perturbed that her eldest son had gone to work instead of sticking around to "get acquainted" with his prospective sister-in-law, she didn't say so.

Both Tadd and Penny were excited about a boat trip, though Tadd was patently disappointed that his new hero wouldn't be available.

"But Mom, why isn't Donovan coming?" he asked, walking into the bathroom as Jodie was braiding Penny's hair. "I thought he liked us."

Jodie's hands shook and she took a calming breath. "Donovan has to work. He owns an air-transit business that takes a lot of time to run. He can't drop everything to escort us around Fairbanks."

Tadd kicked the side of the bathtub. "If he owns it, then why can't he make someone else do the work?" he asked with innocent logic.

"Because he can't." She finished tying the ribbons on the end of Penny's two braids, then motioned to her son. "Let's see if I can get that hair under control. You look like you combed it with an eggbeater."

With a heartfelt sigh, Tadd plopped himself down

on the chair his sister had vacated. "It's just going to stick up again," he said practically.

"Then I—I'll use some of the hair tonic."

Tadd's desolate face brightened. "Dad's stuff?"

Jodie nodded and searched in her cosmetic case for the small travel-size bottle of hair tonic. She turned it over in her hand and sighed. *Dad's stuff.* It was the brand Mark had always used. Tadd loved it when she used the tonic on his hair—it made him feel closer to his father.

Shaking some onto her palm, she braced herself for the onslaught of memories and emotions the scent always provoked, yet nothing happened.

Jodie took a deeper breath and it was the same— a pleasant nostalgic warmth, but not the wrenching pain she'd always felt before.

With a sigh of relief, she ran her fingers through Tadd's dark hair and combed it into place. "There. I'm lucky to have such a handsome guy to take me places," she murmured.

"Aw, Mom," Tadd protested, but he was pleased. She could see it in his eyes and the heightened color beneath his olive-toned skin.

"Go ahead. I'll be out in a minute," Jodie said.

"Are you okay?" he asked, growing more solemn. Sometimes he was too grown-up, as though he'd never been a child at all.

She smiled a reassurance. "Fine." When he disappeared she looked at the bottle of hair tonic again. She wasn't even sure why she'd brought the bottle to Alaska, except that Tadd would have been upset.

Still curious, she sniffed the open container. It *did* remind her of Mark, but that was all. Just a reminder, like looking back on a summer day at the beach.

"Jodie?" Evelyn said, putting her head around the half-open door. "Is everything all right? Tadd thought you might be upset."

Jodie shook her head and tossed the bottle back in her case. A part of her felt freer than she'd felt in years. "Nope, I'm fine."

Evelyn nodded without saying anything, but her eyes spoke volumes. Tadd had probably said something about his father, and Evelyn would be understandably concerned since she hoped Jodie would marry Cole.

A stab of remorse hit Jodie as she followed her hostess back to the kitchen. The possibility of marrying Cole was growing remote. How could she marry one brother when she had a burning awareness of the other?

It was too strange, too much like a soap opera, to work. She wanted a simple, uncomplicated marriage, not something fit for a daytime drama on television.

Shamus looked up as they walked in, and he took a last swallow of his tea. "Ready to go, Jodie love?"

Jodie smiled and nodded. If nothing else, they'd met some wonderful people. And she'd discovered her shattered heart had healed more than she'd ever expected.

It was worth the trip, even if she didn't get married.

When Donovan got up the next morning, he found his mother sitting in the kitchen, as if waiting for him to appear.

"Morning," he said, kissing her forehead.

"Good morning." She looked at him critically. "You didn't come home last night."

"Of course I came home. I'm here, aren't I?" Donovan squirmed nonetheless, because he knew what she meant. He'd left the previous morning before anyone was awake, and returned after he figured everyone was in bed. He poured a cup of coffee and leaned against the counter. "I had work to do at the office."

"You missed a good day. We took the riverboat up the Chena River. It was fun, but Tadd was disappointed you couldn't come."

Donovan thought about the youngster and realized he would have enjoyed spending the day with both Tadd and Penny. Hell, for that matter he would have enjoyed spending the time with Jodie...except for his permanent state of arousal whenever she was around.

"Sorry."

"Those are the nicest children," his mother mused with a fond smile. "I adore them both. Penny is so sweet, and Tadd is smart and funny."

Great. Donovan sighed inwardly. His mother was falling in love with the kids, anticipating having them as grandchildren. He had to warn her, before she got too fond of the entire Richards family.

"Mom," he murmured, sitting down and covering her hand with his own, "the other night at Cole's...I found something that might change things."

Her expression dimmed. "Found what?"

"Some letters Cole tried to write. I think he's changed his mind about getting married."

"But he didn't stop Jodie from coming," Evelyn protested. "He said he still wanted to marry her. That doesn't make any sense."

Donovan didn't repeat his opinion that *marriage* didn't make sense. His mother knew all about his opinions, and he was getting mixed up about it anyway. He wished he could get away, to sort everything out in his head.

"I just don't want you getting too fond of the children," he said. "From what I could tell, it looks like Cole didn't know how to break things off. Maybe he decided to tell her face-to-face."

Evelyn's face grew thoughtful. "You're sure?"

"Pretty much."

"Well, we can't say anything. I mean, you *could* be wrong," she said. "And Cole should tell Jodie himself if that's what he's decided. Promise you won't say anything to her?"

"I...guess."

The sound of a door opening caused them both to freeze, and it wasn't until Shamus appeared that Donovan took a full breath. He was relieved to leave any truth-telling to Cole. It would be too damned uncomfortable admitting that his brother had brought Jodie and the children to Alaska without intending to go through with the wedding.

That is...*if* Cole had changed his mind. There was a remote possibility he'd only had a momentary case of cold feet.

The image of those scribbled letters rose in Donovan's mind and he sighed.

No. They'd been written over a period time, with

different dates at the top, and a variety of multiple, faltering explanations and excuses.

"Will you come out to the kennel with me?" Shamus asked, breaking into Donovan's thoughts. "I want to feed the dogs so we can get an early start. We're taking Jodie and the young'uns to one of the gold mines today."

Donovan looked at his stepfather and nodded. "Fine."

As they walked across the yard to the barn, Shamus put a hand on his shoulder. "How are you doing, lad?" he murmured.

"Fine."

"Really?" The older man looked at him, obviously seeing the effects of three restless nights in a row on his stepson's face.

"No, not really. I kissed Jodie," Donovan found himself admitting. "The other night at Cole's. I know it was a mistake, but I can't stop thinking about it."

"And...Cole?"

"Cole is probably out of the picture," Donovan said, then explained about the letters he'd found. "I still feel guilty, but that isn't the problem. Not really."

Shamus nodded gravely. "Aye. Evie says you don't believe in marriage."

"Yeah." Donovan pulled two blocks of meat from the kennel freezer, handing the first to his stepfather. Together they chopped it into pieces with hatchets, accompanied by the excited yips and whines of the sled dogs in their fenced runs. More food than usual was needed, since Shamus was also caring for Cole's team during his climb on McKinley.

"There now, stop fussin'. You'll have plenty." Shamus gave each dog its portion, along with a kind word. The animals looked at him adoringly before tearing into the icy meal. Sled dogs had iron jaws— their teeth made short work of even the hardest frozen chunks of meat.

Together they cleaned the chopping table and locked the hatchets back into the cabinet. After several minutes of silence, Donovan cleared his throat. Ever since his discussion with Jodie about his father's desertion, he'd had a question to ask Shamus.

"Jodie said something the other day, and it got me to thinking."

"Aye?"

"She…" Donovan's voice trailed off, then he looked his stepfather squarely in the eye. "Would you have ever walked out on us, like my dad?"

If the question surprised Shamus, he didn't show it. He simply shook his head. "No, lad."

"How do you know?"

"Because it would be easier to cut out my heart. You're my family, and a man worth his name takes care of his family."

Donovan opened his mouth, but the back door of the house slammed and Tadd came barreling into the yard, with Jodie following at a slower pace.

"Did you feed them already?" Tadd asked breathlessly.

"Aye, except for Keeta, here," Shamus said, patting the husky who sat patiently at his side. Keeta was a truly ancient husky who'd long since lost her teeth. These days she mostly sat in a warm corner

of the house and slept. "She needs the canned food.
Do you remember where I keep it?"

Tadd nodded self-importantly. "I remember."

"I hope Tadd isn't getting in the way," Jodie
said, avoiding Donovan's gaze.

"Not at all, lass."

With a kind smile, Shamus followed Tadd into
the barn used to house the sled team's needs.

"I'll go help Evelyn," Jodie murmured, backing
away from Donovan.

"I'm not going to bite," he said, a little irritated.
"So you don't have to run off just because I'm
here."

Jodie looked at him and sighed. "We agreed we
should avoid each other."

"Well, we can't. Mom expects me to go along
today." Even as the words left his mouth, Donovan
groaned silently. His mother hadn't said any such
thing. It was his own pathetic excuse to see Jodie
and spend time with her.

Instead of warning his mother, he should have
warned himself.

"Oh."

Jodie put a hand to her throat. She hadn't expected to see Donovan, except in passing. It was
what they'd agreed on.

"I thought...that is, we weren't going to—"

"Spend time together?" Donovan nodded. "But
I can't be rude to my own mother. Besides..." He
gave her a breathtaking smile. "I love panning for
gold. There's nothing like finding a shiny little nugget hiding in a load of wet gravel."

"I didn't realize we'd be panning for gold," Jodie
said, surprised.

He gave her another maddening, utterly charming smile. "We can't let you come to Fairbanks and *not* pan for gold. It'll be fun. Just wait and see."

Donovan strolled back into the house while Jodie wrapped her arms around herself and shivered. But she wasn't cold. It was mostly a sensation like standing on the edge of a cliff—an awareness of danger, a hint of excitement and a whole lot of wondering how you got there.

She'd thought it was settled—she and Donovan would avoid each other as much as possible. Now they were all spending the day together and she was actually excited about it.

It's the smile, Jodie decided. A warm, carefree smile that said he enjoyed life. She'd lost the ability to have fun, so watching Donovan was an education.

Klondike pushed his nose against her and she paused to rub his nose.

"I can't keep you," she murmured. "It wouldn't be right if I don't marry Cole."

The husky pup cocked his head to one side and yipped. He was sweet and cuddly and she wished he really *did* belong to her, but he was too valuable as a sled dog to be given to a stranger. Klondike belonged on a sled team—either Cole's team, or the one belonging to his stepfather.

Her jaw tightening, Jodie stood and yanked at the hem of her shorts. Mushing was another thing Cole had failed to discuss in his letters. Maybe she *should* have read that blasted report from the private investigator. Then she'd have known more about the man she was supposedly going to marry.

From the corner of her eye she saw Donovan walk back onto the porch. He leaned his elbows on the porch rail and gazed at Mount McKinley, his jeans drawn tight over muscled thighs.

Thoughts of Cole vanished from Jodie's mind. She'd never been the kind of woman to salivate over a man's rear end, but Donovan's entire body was awe-inspiring. She'd have to be dead not to appreciate it.

The memory of his urgent arousal pressed against her abdomen brought a moan to Jodie's throat and she closed her eyes. She had to get a grip on herself. Practical, sensible women with two children did not lose their perspective because of a man's killer sex appeal.

She looked at Donovan again and found him watching her.

"Can't make up your mind?" he asked softly.

Startled, Jodie's mouth dropped opened. He didn't know, did he? What she'd been thinking about? Or rather, what she'd almost thought...that maybe she should have made love with him. That maybe she should have thrown caution and discipline to the wind and enjoyed the moment.

"Make up my mind?"

He gave her that maddening smile again. "About coming inside. You've been just standing there for at least five minutes."

Heat burned in Jodie's face. She probably looked like an idiot. Okay, so the man was reasonably sexy. There wasn't any reason to get carried away with herself and make a mistake she'd always regret.

Or was it a bigger mistake *not* getting carried away with herself?

Chapter Eight

"Having fun?"

"What do you think?" Jodie returned, smiling at Donovan. At the moment she didn't have a care in the world. The sun was shining, it was warm and the day held a magical enchantment, like going to an amusement park.

Real time didn't exist in amusement parks—it just divided and flowed around you like an ancient river. That's how she felt about a day with Donovan Masters—like she'd gone to a big, grand amusement park. He had an amazing capacity for carefree enjoyment.

"Com'on, Donovan," Tadd said. He waved a large, shallow pan in the air. "Show me how to do it."

The tour at the gold mine included a choice of panning for gold out of a sluice box, or from the creek. Naturally her adventuresome son had selected the creek.

"I'll teach you once he gets the hang of it," Donovan murmured. He took off his shoes and socks and rolled his jeans up his legs.

Jodie stretched and smiled sleepily. "Don't hurry."

"Then stop looking like that," he said. His tone had become rougher, more intimate, and she blinked in surprise.

"Like what?"

"Like you just woke up. It makes a man think."

The breath caught in Jodie's throat. In the sunlight, Donovan's brown eyes contained their own golden flecks, but his pupils had dilated, erasing the gold. "I didn't mean to look...any particular way."

"I know. That's what makes it worse." His grin was lopsided. "You don't flirt or tease, or do one damn thing to turn me on."

He spread out the quilt he'd carried down from the car, then turned on his heel. For a full minute Jodie just stared. She couldn't decide if she'd just been insulted or complimented, or a little of both.

No, she didn't flirt; she didn't know how, so any flirting was purely accidental. An adolescent girl with no mother and four older brothers learned to be direct. There hadn't been any other way to survive, particularly with the general as her father. General McBride didn't have a subtle bone in his body.

She spread the quilt on the ground and stretched out on it, getting sleepy all over again. Penny had fallen asleep over a late lunch, so Shamus and Evelyn had put her down in the Jeep for a nap, insisting on watching her while the rest of the party panned for gold.

If Jodie didn't know better, she'd think Evelyn

was trying her hand at matchmaking. A couple of times Jodie had seen the older woman watching her and Donovan, a speculative look in her eyes. Even if Evelyn did have something in mind, it wouldn't do her any good. Neither party was interested...at least not much. And certainly not in a permanent arrangement.

Jodie tucked her hand behind her head, listening to the gurgle of water and the happy sounds of vacationers as they tried to find gold in the creek's gravel. There were fewer people than up at the rows of sluice boxes, but it wasn't private. If Evelyn had matchmaking in mind, the atmosphere was hardly conducive to fostering romance.

Turning on her side, Jodie watched as Donovan crouched, teaching Tadd how to swirl the water and sand in the pan. He was patient and laughed often, taking the occasional splashes of creek water in his stride.

"But how can it work?" Tadd asked. "Those rocks are bigger than those tiny bits of gold they showed us at the mine."

"Gold is really heavy, so when you swirl the water and sand around, it sifts out and falls to the bottom," Donovan explained. "You move the water fast enough to wash off the lighter stuff, but not so fast it dumps everything out."

"That's how the sluice box works?"

"Yup. It has little cleats on the bottom to catch the gold as the water moves down the box. Panning is backbreaking work, and the sluice box made it a little easier and faster for the early miners."

Jodie could only see their backs as they worked, but the warm timbre of Donovan's voice crept through her and she closed her eyes. He really seemed to enjoy being around the children. Penny still called him "Daddy," and they'd given up convincing her to stop. Of course, that was mostly because she'd started crying the last time, and Donovan had a weakness when it came to Penny's tears.

In other men Jodie might have suspected he was being nice to her children to impress her. She was used to men having ulterior motives, especially the men under her father's command. They might like her and the kids, but they were also interested in impressing General McBride.

Not Donovan. He was nice to her family because he liked them, not for any other reason.

"Hey, wake up," Donovan said, interrupting her train of thought.

"I'm not asleep."

"You sure look like it."

Jodie opened her eyes and looked at him standing nearby, his legs set apart in a wide stance. He towered above her, aggressively male, and a shaft of warmth slid through her tummy.

"What if I want to sleep?" she asked, her breath coming faster.

"You can't. I have to teach you to pan for gold." He motioned with the second pan they'd brought from the main visitor's area of the mine.

"You do, huh?"

"It's my duty as an Alaskan."

She thought about it. Surely she couldn't get into too much trouble panning for gold on a semipublic creek, with her son just a few feet away. She put her arm up, too relaxed to care if it gave him ideas. "Okay. Pull me up."

Donovan pulled her upright. "I wouldn't do that for just anyone," he said, putting his hands on her waist to steady her.

"Just anyone who asks."

His smile was purely male. "Not exactly."

Jodie looked away quickly. She might have been wrong about getting in trouble. Donovan liked to touch. It was a quality she normally would appreciate, but it wasn't good in a man she wasn't going to marry or date, or even kiss again.

"So, is Tadd going to strike it rich?" she asked.

They both looked up the creek where Tadd was intently leaning over and swishing water around his pan. He worked with a single-minded focus that excluded everything but him, the water and the pan he held.

"He'll get some gold," Donovan said confidently.

"Oh? Why so sure?"

"I just am."

Jodie hid a smile. She'd seen Donovan buy a sample of gold flakes and dust from one of the miners and knew he'd salt Tadd's pan if necessary. She tapped her forefinger on his shirt pocket, knowing it was where he'd hidden the small plastic bag containing the gold.

"That's cheating."

"Not if you're eight years old. You're entitled to dreams when you're eight."

There was a dark flicker of pain in his eyes that vanished, almost as quickly as it had come. Jodie knew without saying that he was remembering his childhood, the years of being too young to help his mom through the rough times.

What had he said? As a child he'd stolen a coat for her? He was such an honorable man, it probably still bothered him knowing he'd done something against his nature. Even to help his mother.

"Donovan..."

He looked down at her and shook his head. "Never mind, Jodie." He gave her waist a gentle squeeze before stepping away. "Let's pan for some gold."

At the edge of the creek Jodie kicked off her shoes. The bank was just high enough that it wasn't possible for her to kneel or crouch on the edge and still reach the water. She stepped into the shallow current, then instantly hopped out again.

"It's cold!" she protested.

"Tenderfoot."

Jodie swung around and glared. "I heard that."

"You were supposed to." Donovan gave her a teasing grin. "Now get back in the creek like a good little tenderfoot, and I'll figure out a way of keeping you warm. Real warm. You'll be so warm, you'll need the water to cool off." He wiggled his eyebrows with mock lechery and Jodie laughed.

"Even *you* wouldn't do that in public," she said, inching back into the icy creek. "And we're supposed to be ignoring those impulses. Remember?"

Donovan sighed and had trouble remembering anything except his need to touch Jodie. He'd known he was going to tempt fate again—knew it from the moment he'd said he was going to the gold mine. He'd known he wouldn't let anyone else teach her to pan for gold, and that he could maneuver the teaching into some very pleasant contact.

She leaned over, peering intently into the flowing

current. Her bottom was snugly encased in a pair of green shorts and looked like an inverted heart. Donovan dragged in a breath of air. She'd felt so good in his hands the other night. He could still feel the firm warmth of her curves in the palms of his hands.

"I heard some of what you told Tadd," Jodie said, still looking into the water. "It's a miracle anyone found gold doing this." She pulled up a fistful of sand and let it sift through her fingers, looking between it, and the pan, with equal disbelief.

"It's hard work, that's for sure." Donovan glanced down the creek. Tadd had drifted more than thirty feet away. "Tadd, that's far enough," he called.

The boy nodded without looking up. He used a small shovel to dig more gravel into his pan, then began dipping and swirling it again.

"You've given my son gold fever," Jodie said lightly, then her expression grew more serious. "It's safe out here, isn't it? I know there are bears, even this close to Fairbanks."

"I've been watching," Donovan assured her. "Are you ready to learn panning?"

"Hmm."

It was a noncommittal comment, but Donovan decided she wasn't saying no, and that was all that counted. He took the gold pan and scooped up some sand from the creek bottom. "Ready?"

He gave Jodie the pan, then stepped behind her. Putting his hands over hers, he demonstrated the proper circular motion, enjoying each innocent bump and grind of her bottom against him.

"Are you sure this is the way to find gold?" she asked dryly. "Without any water?"

"It's just practice. You need to know what motion to use. You can go ahead now and scoop some water in the pan." He was playing with fire, but like a child fascinated with a hot, bright flame, he couldn't turn away.

Donovan drew a deep breath as Jodie filled her pan and straightened. The lesson was plainly harder on him than her, and he was having second thoughts about the wisdom of touching her.

Actually, he'd known how dangerous it was to get his hands on Jodie, he'd just ignored the danger.

"A firm, but gentle motion," he said, showing her again. "You have to be careful or you'll get doused."

"I—*yikes*," Jodie yelped abruptly, stumbling backward. Donovan hadn't anticipated the movement, but he twisted so they landed on the bank, rather than in the creek. She looked at him, then looked down at the water sloshed from her shoulders to her knees. "You mean like that?"

"Yeah, like that." Donovan was having trouble breathing. The contact with cold creek water had tightened Jodie's nipples into hard, crinkled points, and the thin cotton of her shirt did nothing to conceal the condition. His own body tightened with alarming speed and he edged a couple of feet away.

"I'll get this right," Jodie said. She got up and scooped more water into the pan. Now that she was used to it, the water felt refreshing in the eighty-five degree heat. "Which direction is best?" she asked.

"Doesn't matter."

The hoarseness of Donovan's voice broke her concentration and she glanced up. He was standing next to her, though he hadn't put his arms around her again.

"Go ahead, don't mind me," he growled. His eyes were focused on her chest.

Looking back down, Jodie gulped. She plucked the front of her shirt away from her breasts, more embarrassed than she'd thought possible. "Uh…women are at a distinct disadvantage at times like this," she mumbled.

"That depends on where you're standing."

Jodie hastily concentrated on the pan. She wasn't interested in finding gold, but in surviving the sensual heat in Donovan's face. She scooped more sand and water into the pan, then resumed a swirling motion.

"You must think I'm a jerk," he muttered after a few minutes of silence.

"Why is that?"

He sat on the grass and ran his fingers through his hair. "You're engaged to Cole, but I still kissed you. I still *want* you."

Jodie swirled the pan another couple times, paying little attention to the process. She knew men took their honor seriously, sometimes to a ridiculous degree. It could be both sweet and irritating.

"I don't think you're a jerk," she said.

"I kissed you."

"It was mutual. We kissed each other." Sighing, Jodie sat next to Donovan and balanced the wet gold pan on her legs. "I meant what I said—I don't owe Cole anything. And besides, I'm not really engaged to Cole, we're just talking about it."

"But you're upset he went on the climb." Donovan stared at the opposite bank of the creek. "And you have every right to be furious. Climbing Mount McKinley might be Cole's dream, but he should have settled his priorities before asking you to come here.''

She couldn't honestly disagree. "I'm not angry anymore," she said. "I may have a temper, but it cools off quickly."

"Lucky Cole." Donovan's tone was half frustration, half baffled anger.

"You sound almost jealous."

"Maybe I am."

Jodie sighed. She looked to see where Tadd had gone, and saw him still panning in the creek, well out of easy hearing distance. "That isn't logical," she said.

Donovan threw out his hand. "Don't you think I know that?"

"Just checking."

The humorous edge in Jodie's voice sent a quaking awareness through Donovan. She didn't know the half of it. He was jealous even though he didn't want to get married himself. He was jealous of his brother, even though Cole probably wasn't going to marry Jodie. And he was jealous because Cole might take one look at her and forget he'd ever changed his mind.

The whole thing was more than complicated, it was a nightmare.

Donovan leaned back on one elbow and considered his actions over the past several days. He wasn't a jealous sort of guy. Once he would have said he didn't have a possessive bone in his body. Win some, lose some—that was his basic philosophy when it came to women. If you never planned to get married or have a long-term relationship, you could be blasé about casual girlfriends moving in and out of your life.

Then Jodie had arrived and blown his theories to kingdom come.

For the first time in his life he had to deal with wanting a woman he couldn't have. A permanent kind of woman, with children and a yen for a wedding ring. Maybe if Jodie wanted to fall in love and get married, it might be different. Except she didn't want to fall in love, she wanted something nice and safe and unemotional.

Maybe if Jodie wanted to fall in love...

He broke out in a cold sweat.

What was he thinking? Love wouldn't make any difference. Heck, he'd decided her idea of a mail-order marriage was relatively sensible, so it was crazy to start thinking the opposite.

"You're sort of pale. Are you okay?" Jodie asked.

"Fine." Donovan rubbed his face. His opinion about love hadn't changed, any more than his opinion about marriage had changed. Right? Sure, Jodie was as close to perfect as a potential wife could get, but that didn't make her perfect for him.

Besides, what would happen if she changed her mind about living in Alaska? She'd lived here as a child, but that didn't guarantee she'd enjoy the realities of freezing weather and practically no daylight during the winter. After a year or two she might decide to pull up stakes and leave. Then her husband would have to decide if he was staying or going with her.

"I'm not leaving Alaska," Donovan muttered.

Confusion replaced the concern in Jodie's green eyes. "I don't understand. Why would you think about leaving? You grew up here."

He took several deep breaths. "No reason. I was just thinking about a—a business deal," he said.

"I don't know why anyone would leave." Jodie stretched and looked around the sun-dappled creek. "Even if things don't work out with Cole, we're still moving to Alaska," she said, giving Donovan a small sideways glance. She might as well lay the groundwork, so he wouldn't think she was pursuing him later.

"Oh?"

"Probably to Anchorage. Since it's where we lived when I was a kid, that would make more sense. But I haven't really made up my mind. Juneau might be nice, too."

"Mom and Shamus will be disappointed. I'm sure they'll want you closer."

She lifted her shoulders in a small shrug. "Fairbanks would be awkward if I—I don't marry Cole. Your folks might prefer us to be somewhere else."

Donovan caught her elbow, pulling her around to face him. "You don't really believe that, do you? They'd adopt you if they could, and it has nothing to do with my brother. They're crazy about both you and the kids."

Jodie flicked the tip of her tongue over her lips, then blushed at Donovan's sudden, avid focus on her mouth. She hadn't been flirting, but the result was the same. "I'm...crazy about them, too. They're very special."

Lifting his hand, he traced the moisture her tongue had left, then threaded his fingers through her hair. "Why do all my good intentions fly out the window when I'm around you?" he asked roughly.

"Don't," she whispered as he leaned closer. "We agreed not to do this again."

"Right. *Cole*."

"We both know I'm not going to marry Cole," Jodie said quietly, finally admitting what she'd known in her heart for the last two days.

"Do we know that?"

"Yes." She tugged his hand away from her hair, only to find her fingers laced with Donovan's and resting on his thigh.

"Then why?"

"I wasn't…entirely honest the other night."

Donovan's eyebrows shot upward. "About what?" His thumb stroked her palm and she shivered. They were just holding hands. It should have been friendly, not so intimate.

"When you asked why I thought we weren't compatible, and that you figured it was more than the way we felt about marriage."

"I remember. You said I was too much like your first husband."

Jodie closed her eyes, unable to look at him while she explained. "It's because I *could* fall in love with you, and I don't want to."

"That would definitely have complicated things if you became my sister-in-law," Donovan said in a conversational tone and Jodie's eyes shot open.

"I shouldn't have told you," she said, annoyed. "I didn't say that I *was* in love with you, just that I'm being careful to avoid the problem."

"Too bad there isn't a vaccine for problems like that."

"It's certainly not anything *you* have to worry about. You don't even believe in love," Jodie snapped. She pulled her hand free and poked at the contents of the gold pan. She couldn't believe she'd opened her mouth and confessed anything so embarrassing.

"I'm sorry," Donovan said softly. "I didn't mean to be flip, it just threw me. Most women wouldn't have been so honest."

"I'm not like most women."

"That's becoming painfully clear to me."

"Painfully? You sure know how to bolster a woman's ego," Jodie mumbled.

"If you knew how tight my jeans were right now, your ego would feel just fine," he rasped. "You'd know exactly what kind of pain I'm having."

Unable to stop herself, Jodie peeked at the significant portion of Donovan's anatomy. He was right. Her ego did feel better, because those jeans looked ready to burst their seams. It was reassuring and disturbing at the same time, because her body reacted with astonishing speed, becoming warm and pliable at the evidence of his response to her.

"Men are at a distinct disadvantage in situations like this," Donovan said with an attempt at humor. He shifted his legs and grimaced.

"That depends on where you're...uh, sitting." Jodie looked back at her gold pan, still feeling a pleasant tingle.

There were pebbles and large pieces of rock in the pan that should have been sorted out at the beginning, and she idly rolled them around with the tip of her finger. She wasn't paying much attention until she realized the largest pebble wasn't a pebble at all.

Jodie plucked the nugget out and looked at it in surprise. "Isn't this what we've been looking for?"

"We haven't been looking at all," Donovan grumbled. He yanked a tuft of grass from the ground and shredded it with his fingers.

"*Donovan.*"

Something was thrust in front of his face. It was wet and shiny in places, and had the distinct color of gold. "I'll be damned." He took the nugget and balanced it in his palm. "I'll bet it weighs almost a troy ounce."

"I wish Tadd could have found it," Jodie said. She glanced at her son who was still using his pan at the edge of the water. "He would have been so excited."

A curious ache tugged at Donovan's throat. Jodie was sincere—she wished Tadd had found the nugget instead. It was a sweet, generous wish, and he couldn't imagine the women he'd dated over the years being so generous, even with their own children, if they'd had any.

"I could go check on how he's doing, and slip it in when he's not looking."

"And if he catches you, he'll never trust an adult again," Jodie warned. "Besides, he'll get suspicious if he finds it right after you come over. What if we put the nugget back in the creek, then suggest he look in the same place? That wouldn't exactly be cheating, because he'd just be finding it all over again."

Donovan thought for a moment, then shook his

head. "Tadd is too smart. He'll catch on, no matter what we do."

They nodded in glum agreement.

"So much for salting his pan," Donovan murmured, thinking about the gold sample he'd gotten to ensure Tadd wouldn't be disappointed with his mining efforts.

"It was a nice thought," Jodie said, smiling at him. "There aren't many men who would have taken the trouble."

"He's a great kid."

"I think so."

Jodie lifted the hair from the back of her neck, twirling it into a temporary ponytail for coolness. The day was so warm, the water she'd splashed on herself had already dried. Beads of perspiration dampened her face and Donovan had to restrain his hands to keep from touching her. First he wanted to draw her down in the grass, then he wanted to kiss every inch of her beautiful body and after that he could think of some creative uses for cool creek water.

The fit of his jeans went from uncomfortably tight to near strangulation.

How was it that Jodie got more beautiful each time he looked at her? Was it an optical illusion, or just a slow recognition of something he should have seen all along?

Near desperation, Donovan thrust the nugget in Jodie's hand, then grabbed the gold pan and jumped into the creek. He went to the middle and crouched down, swirling the pan with a vicious force. Most people didn't go hip-deep when they were panning, but most people didn't need the cooling effects of the water, either. He was so aroused it hurt to breathe, much less move.

It wasn't just physical though, when Jodie had said he was the kind of man she *could* love, he'd wanted to crow like a rooster.

"Is that a better way of finding gold?" she called.

He gave her a searing glance over his shoulder.

Anything else Jodie wanted to say died in her throat. If Donovan wanted to take the equivalent of a cold shower in the middle of a creek, he probably needed it. The notion gave her a distinct feminine pleasure, and confused her at the same time. Men were impossible to understand.

She rolled the gold nugget around on the palm of her hand. It was pretty, but she still wished Tadd had been the lucky finder. Before she could dwell on the pensive wish, there was an excited shout from her son.

"Oh, *wow*. Mom, Donovan, look what I found." Tadd charged upstream, sending feathers of water in every direction, he had the gold pan clutched in one arm and his fist closed around something. "See? It's gold. Isn't it, Donovan?"

He showed them a smaller version of the nugget Jodie had found, his eyes glowing with delight.

"That's wonderful," Jodie said, giving him a hug.

"It sure is, buddy." Donovan tousled Tadd's hair, then raised his hand for a congratulatory high five.

Smiling, Jodie slipped her own discovery into Donovan's back jeans pocket to keep Tadd from seeing it. The muscles of Donovan's buttocks tensed at the contact and she bit her lip. "Sorry," she whispered.

When Tadd had happily returned to his panning, Donovan turned around and raised his eyebrow. "Why didn't you put it in your own pocket?"

"Yours was more convenient. And I figured he couldn't see my hand behind your back."

"You're determined to kill me, aren't you?"

A faint smile played on her mouth. "Lust is *not* a life-threatening condition."

"Maybe, but I don't want to put it to a test."

Chapter Nine

Jodie drowsed as they drove home, swaying with each movement of the Jeep Grand Cherokee as it turned corners and swung around bends in the road. It was nice to relax. Penny was riding with Shamus and Evelyn, and Tadd was chattering away with Donovan about gold and how much money a fellow could make if he really tried.

"At established mines you'd just work for wages and maybe a small percentage of the profit," Donovan said. "Sometimes you can lease the land or make another arrangement for your own mining operation, but there's never a guarantee you'll find gold."

"Oh." Tadd looked crestfallen. "Didn't a lot of people get rich during the gold rush?"

"Some did. But lots more prospectors barely scraped by, or didn't even make enough to live on."

Jodie yawned and stretched. "Remember what your teacher said about the California gold rush?"

she asked. "It was mostly the merchants selling food to the miners who made fortunes. A dollar for a slice of bread, and another dollar for some butter. A miner would work all day just to buy food."

"I imagine they paid a lot for their entertainment, too," Donovan murmured, a wicked look in his eye and Jodie glared at him.

"I'm sure they did," she said stiffly.

Fortunately, Tadd wasn't interested in a miner's entertainment, just in how much money he could make. "But what if you found a great big piece of gold? You'd be rich, wouldn't you?" He'd been really impressed when the assay office at the mine had assessed his gold find at eighty-five dollars. "Like a thousand times bigger than my nugget?"

"The biggest piece they ever found in Alaska was a little under fourteen pounds," Donovan explained. "You'd make a lot of money, but it's just a fluke to find something that big."

Tadd's mouth dropped open. "Gosh, you'd be like a *billionaire.*"

"Billionaire, eh?" Donovan had trouble keeping a straight face as he glanced at Jodie. "Is that the new math they're teaching in Florida?" he teased.

She rolled her eyes. "Tadd, you didn't want to sell your nugget, so why all the questions?"

"Just wondered."

Donovan knew the reason Tadd was so interested in money—he wanted his mom to have a pair of gold nugget earrings, like the ones he'd seen in the gift shop at the mine. Except he'd only found one nugget. Donovan had offered to help, but Tadd had refused. The boy was stubbornly proud, just like his mother.

Lord. Donovan shook his head. How could he have thought Jodie wanted a husband to get away from her father? She might be a mixture of silk and satin on the outside, but inside she had a backbone made of steel.

He laughed to himself, imagining the sparks that must have flown between her and General McBride. They were probably a lot alike, constantly rubbing each other the wrong way.

"What's so funny?" Jodie asked.

"Private joke."

"Something about expensive entertainment, perhaps? What if he'd asked for details?" she muttered.

Donovan looked in the rearview mirror. Tadd was absorbed in a book on gold mining. "Details about plays and musicals, that kind of thing?" he asked innocently.

"You're a rat. Do you know that?"

"I know, but don't tell Mom. She thinks I'm perfect."

They pulled into the driveway and Donovan saw the sturdy minivan from the Triple M Transit office was parked by the barn. His partners and their families had arrived.

"Hey, Tadd," he said. "You're getting a roommate."

Tadd looked up. "Yeah?"

"See the boy over by the dog run? That's Jamie McCoy, and he's seven years old. I think you'll get along great together."

"Okay."

Jodie looked far more tense than her son, and Donovan gave her hand a squeeze after he'd stopped the Jeep. "You'll like them. They're nice people," he reassured her. Tadd had already jumped out and was headed for the dog run.

"I feel like we're in the way," she said.

"You worry too much. I told you. Mom—"

"Enjoys lots of company," she finished for him. "But it's more than that. It's as if I'm here on false pretenses."

Donovan sighed.

We both know I'm not going to marry Cole.

Jodie hadn't read the letters, but she'd decided on her own that she wasn't marrying Cole. Now she was feeling responsible for something that wasn't her fault. She'd come to Alaska in good faith; it was the two Masters brothers who'd screwed things up.

"Look, Mom knew there was a good chance things wouldn't work out," Donovan said finally. "She knew from the beginning, because of Cole pulling that damned stupid stunt of taking off for McKinley."

"You didn't think the climbing was stupid when you explained at the airport," Jodie reminded him. "You thought he was crazy to contemplate getting married."

"Well, I think he's stupid now." Donovan looked at Jodie, a frustrated expression on his face. "You deserve better. Your kids deserve better."

She didn't say anything and he sighed again.

"Jodie, I may not have any faith in marriage, but that doesn't mean I don't want you to have the best."

She unbuckled the seat belt. "I'm not your problem, Donovan. I can manage very well on my own."

"I know. But believe it or not, I care about you."

"Do you?"

"Yes." The word came out with explosive force, and he counted to ten. "I don't know how we get in these discussions, but it's making me crazy."

"Then we should stop having them." Jodie got out and walked toward Donovan's friends. Her heart was aching, though she couldn't have explained why. The closer she got to Donovan, the harder it was to remember the reasons she shouldn't fall in love with him.

A broken heart, remember?

A man who didn't believe in love or marriage.

The risk of loving and losing again.

Yeah, Jodie agreed silently.

But it was counterbalanced with other considerations. Such as a man her children were wild about. A man who valued simple pleasures. Who generously laughed and teased, reminding her of the girl she'd once been.

A man who could make love with his eyes and his voice.

Everything was a risk. Life was a risk. She'd seen her father shut down after her mother's death, becoming more distant and alone with each passing year. Did she want to be like that? Wasn't it the reason she'd decided to get married again?

"Donovan!"

Startled, Jodie looked up in time to see a flame-haired woman throw herself into Donovan's arms. He was laughing as he hugged her back. "It looks like you got into town early. And by the way, I've only been gone a few days, Callie. Not a year."

"You know my wife….Any excuse to hug somebody," teased another man. He was considerably taller than his petite wife, and he shook hands with

Donovan in a way that left no doubt they were the best of friends.

"Hey, Hannah," Donovan said to a second woman. He bent over the blanket-wrapped baby she held, his voice softening as he stroked the child's cheek. "I think Mary's grown since I've been gone."

"The doctor says she's going to be tall like her daddy." Hannah looked up at the man hovering at her side and he took the opportunity to kiss her.

"I hope that's all she gets from Ross—him being such an ugly cuss." Donovan winked. "If Mary is lucky, she'll have her mama's smile and pretty face."

"You must be talking about some other man," Hannah retorted. "My husband is the most gorgeous man on the planet."

"Except for mine," Callie objected.

The three men chuckled. The comfortable camaraderie was obviously the result of a long friendship and Jodie felt a twinge of wistful envy. Her life as an air force brat, then wife, was a long series of short-lived friendships, each ending when they moved to a new base in a new corner of the world.

The flame-haired woman smiled at Jodie. "Hi. I'm Callie Fitzpatrick, and this is my husband, Mike." She motioned to the man who'd teased her about hugging Donovan. "You must be Tadd's mother—we just met him."

"Yes, Jodie Richards. My daughter is with Evelyn and Shamus, but they're not back yet." She frowned as she looked up the driveway, concern flashing through her mind.

"Don't worry, Jodie," Donovan said quietly.

"Mom mentioned they needed to stop at the store—she was expecting everyone to show up this afternoon and she wanted to be sure there was plenty of milk and stuff. I thought you heard her tell me."

"Oh. I overreact, don't I?"

"If Penny was my daughter, I'd overreact, too." He smiled before turning to Callie. "Where are your two monsters, Callie?"

Callie swatted his arm, at the same time laughing. "Harry and Elijah are taking naps in the house. And they're not monsters."

"That's what every mother says."

"You must think we're terrible," Hannah said to Jodie. She seemed to have a more peaceful personality than her bubbling friend, though Jodie had instantly liked them both.

"No. But I'm a little…envious," Jodie admitted.

"Envious?"

"You're all such close friends. My father was an air force officer, then I married an air force pilot. I've lived on practically every continent, but we never stayed in a place long enough to get to know anyone that well."

"Heavens, all those places sound exciting. I'd never been out of Alaska until I married Ross. We grew up in the same little town down on the panhandle."

Jodie tried to put together the pieces of information she'd learned about Donovan's friends. She knew Ross and Hannah had two children; the oldest was a son by Ross's first marriage. And she had several brothers. "Uhm…Donovan mentioned that you raised six brothers?"

"Yes, my mother died when I was fourteen." The

baby whimpered and Hannah gently rocked her back and forth. "This little one is getting ready for her supper," she said.

"My youngest is only two," Jodie murmured. "But I already miss having a baby in the house."

"They're wonderful, aren't they?" Hannah's face glowed as she watched the fussing infant.

"Is she sleeping through the night yet? It took Penny a long time, but I'd had problems with the pregnancy and her digestion was touchy."

"Mary's up to six hours now. We've only had a couple of rounds with colic." Hannah adjusted the blanket, then kissed her daughter's forehead. "It was different with my youngest brother. I don't think he stopped crying from the day he was born until he was two years old. I still tease him about it—you'd be amazed how embarrassed a grown man can get about a thing like that."

Jodie grinned. "My brothers are all older than me, so I don't have any handy baby stories to tease them about."

"It must be nice having big brothers."

She grimaced. "Yes and no. They're a lot like my father, which means they think they know what's best for everyone. It can be very annoying."

"You must argue a lot."

"You have no idea. It used to sound like World War III in our house." Jodie softened her tart retort with a grin. She wanted to hold the baby, but she was a virtual stranger to Hannah and knew she wouldn't have handed Penny to a stranger, either.

"Mom, can Tadd and I fly the kite?" The interruption came from a boy who was a mirror image of Ross McCoy.

"Jodie, this is my son, Jamie," Hannah said. Supporting the baby with one arm, she brushed her stepson's hair from his forehead with the same loving warmth she'd shown to her daughter and husband. "And yes, you and Tadd *may* fly the kite. Ask your papa to get it for you."

"Thanks, Mom." The youngster took off, with Tadd following close behind.

Hannah turned back to Jodie. "I'm glad he has someone near his age to play with. The other children are too young."

"It's good for Tadd, too."

Jodie's head was spinning with all the names and faces, yet she felt an instant kinship with them. As Donovan had said, they were nice people.

"You flew from Kachelak today?" she asked Hannah as they climbed the porch steps.

"Yes. I talked to Evelyn this morning and she said you were visiting one of the gold mines for the day, but to make ourselves comfortable if we got here first."

"That sounds like Evelyn."

Inside the house it was quieter, and Hannah sat down to nurse the baby. After a couple of minutes Ross came in, his gaze entirely focused on his wife and child.

"Is she eating well? The flight didn't upset her too much? I know the doctor said it would be all right, but she's so little."

Hannah smiled. "She's fine. Don't worry so much."

They shared a lingering kiss and Jodie used the opportunity to slip away. When Hannah and Ross looked at each other, it was like the rest of the world disappeared.

It was beautiful, yet it made Jodie restless. Her marriage had never been like that. Mark's passion for reckless speed was always between them, something she couldn't share, no matter how hard she'd tried.

Sighing, Jodie took her purse into the bedroom, then stood at the window, gazing at the hillside falling away in a patchwork of birch and aspen trees.

"You look lonely in here."

Jodie blinked, for a moment thinking she'd imagined the calm voice, then she turned and saw Donovan standing at the door. He was solid and real and she could feel her heart reaching toward him, no matter how hard she tried to stop it.

"I wanted to leave Hannah and Ross alone when she was...uh, nursing Mary." Jodie didn't know how uncomfortable Donovan might be about the realities of motherhood, but after a moment she shrugged away the concern. He was a grown man. He wouldn't faint with shock at the notion of a woman breast-feeding her child.

"That was considerate."

"Not that they'd notice anyone else in the room," Jodie said wryly.

"They don't mean to be rude."

"Not rude. Just...in love."

Donovan walked toward her. "And there isn't much love in a mail-order marriage. Right?"

Irritation skidded through Jodie and she turned back to the window. She didn't want to talk to Donovan. Whenever they talked, they got tangled up in things they couldn't change or fix. It was like walking on broken glass, and she couldn't take much more.

"Jodie?" He was so close she could feel the heat from his body.

"I thought we were going to stop having 'these discussions.'"

"So I was wrong."

She turned to him. "Nothing has changed in the last hour. Yes, I'm a little envious of what Ross and Hannah have together, but not enough to risk falling in love."

"But you've decided not to marry Cole."

"That's right." Jodie glared at Donovan. "I'm not marrying Cole. Doesn't that make you happy? Aren't you thrilled your little brother won't get caught in the marriage trap?"

"Stop that," he hissed. "Say it. I'm the reason you changed your mind. I messed everything up."

"What do you think? Oh, this is *pointless*. I don't want to talk about it again."

"No." Donovan grabbed her arm before she could escape. "I'm not any happier about what you do to me, than you're happy about the way I make you feel, but we can't pretend it doesn't exist."

"What difference does it make?" Jodie asked dully.

"Dammit. I should never have touched you. I should have left Fairbanks that first day. I wish…"

I wish I'd never met you.

The unspoken words hung in the air.

Donovan could reveal Cole's change of mind about the marriage, but it wouldn't make him less guilty. It wouldn't change the way they were hurting. Ultimately it didn't matter what his brother had decided.

Jodie shook herself, seeing the anger and self-condemnation in Donovan's eyes.

"It isn't your fault. I wouldn't have married Cole, even if he'd been the one to meet me," she whispered. "Sooner or later I would have realized it wasn't right for either of us."

"You're sure about that?"

"I'm sure." She shrugged. "I made a mistake. I'm certain it won't be the last time."

"*Jodie*," Donovan breathed, aching with regret and a longing he couldn't understand. He'd distrusted love and marriage most of his life, but she almost made him believe in fairy tales and happy endings again.

In a way, he'd always blamed himself for his father's desertion, distrusting love and marriage because of it. And now Donovan had to wonder if what he really distrusted was his own judgment— his own ability to love, and be loved.

The commotion outside the bedroom increased. Children ran up and down the hall. Footsteps sounded in the little-used second floor of the house. There were too many people around for quiet conversations and soul-searching, but he couldn't back off. Not yet.

"What you said before…?" Donovan murmured. "That you *could* fall in love with me?"

"Don—"

"No." He put his finger on her lips. "It means a lot, Jodie. You're a special woman and I'm honored you see something in me…that you could love."

"You didn't seem pleased at the time."

"Men don't handle compliments easily."

Jodie looked into Donovan's eyes, recognizing once more the small child who'd been hurt by his father. *I'm honored you see something in me...that you could love.* Despite all the protests, his professed lack of faith in love, was he asking for the very thing he denied existed?

Jump, her heart whispered.

Love him.

Give him what he needs, even if he doesn't know it.

Confused, Jodie drew a ragged breath. She was standing on the edge of a cliff, and there wasn't a parachute in sight. No safety net at the bottom. Nothing to hold her back except invisible threads of fear. And she knew instinctively that losing Donovan could wound her soul irreparably. Mark had never shared all of himself, so there were parts of her that were never shared. It wouldn't be that way with Donovan.

With Donovan, it would be all or nothing.

"Mommmm," shouted Tadd's demanding voice, startling them both. "Shamus says I have to ask if I can go with him and Jamie when he walks the dogs. Can I?" His footsteps thundered down the hall and into the bedroom.

Jodie wasn't in any condition to remind her son of the proper English he should have used, but she was grateful for the reprieve.

"Can I go?" he begged a second time. "Please, Mom. Jamie's mom says it's okay."

"Yes."

"Thanks. You wanna go, too, Donovan?" Tadd asked.

The muscles in Donovan's throat moved convulsively as he swallowed. "Yeah, that sounds great, Tadd. A walk sounds…great."

Donovan strode along, watching the two boys as they raced ahead through the muskeg. He'd warned Tadd and Jamie to avoid the wetter spots, but he knew they might forget. Boys developed amnesia when they got excited.

He wouldn't mind developing amnesia himself.

He'd hurt Jodie. If he stayed in Fairbanks, he'd hurt her even more, which meant he should leave.

Except he couldn't. Like a moth being drawn to a flame, he was drawn to Jodie for reasons he didn't even understand. Not that some of the reasons weren't obvious. Her silky little body was a definite magnet. She had a quick mind and a buried sensuality that challenged him.

"You chewing on something, lad?" Shamus asked, easily matching him stride for stride.

Donovan glanced at his stepfather. "Jodie isn't going to marry Cole."

The older man nodded. "Aye. Evie told me about the letters you found. She's vexed with the boy, but she also knows Cole isn't the right man for Jodie."

"I know. It's obvious she thinks *I'm* the right man for Jodie."

"Are you?"

Donovan paused at the crest of a hill and gazed down at Tadd and Jamie as they played with the dogs. In the past he would have dismissed the question because he didn't feel that close to his stepfather.

But something had changed.

Jodie had forced him to see Shamus in a new way. It wasn't something Donovan was willing to say aloud yet, but it was almost like having a father again.

"Jodie is special, but I'm not sure about marriage," Donovan murmured. "How do you know it's going to work? It's like taking a shot in the dark and hoping you'll find the target."

"Love helps. You know you'll never give up, because it's too important. You build a marriage day by day, tending it like a garden. It isn't a place for silent neglect."

"Love." Donovan thrust his hands in his pockets, remembering the times his dad had said he loved them. And Jodie, saying it was a flaw in the man, not love. "I've spent a long time distrusting that particular emotion," he admitted.

"And Jodie is afraid of it," Shamus said quietly.

Startled, Donovan looked at his stepfather. "She told you?"

"You can see it in her eyes...when she looks at you, lad. You make her feel things she never planned to feel again. It reminds me of your mother. She was a tad stubborn in the beginning, but I wore her down."

Donovan would never underestimate Shamus Carney again. "So how did you change her mind?" he asked.

Shamus clasped Donovan's shoulder in a warm, friendly grip. "Patience, my boy." His eyes twinkled. "Mixed with some Irish stubbornness, of course."

"Of course."

*   *   *

When Jodie stopped shaking, she squared her shoulders and marched out of the bedroom. She'd never hidden in her life, and she wasn't about to start now. Besides, she must have misread Donovan. He'd always been clear how he felt about love between a man and woman. How he felt about marriage.

Too much of a crapshoot to be worth the chance.

Donovan had returned from his walk with the boys and was talking with Mike and Callie, so Jodie sat on the steps and watched him. His partners were attractive, but there was something about Donovan that appealed to her in a way she couldn't explain.

After a couple of minutes Callie smiled over at Jodie, then walked across the yard and sat next to her. "You look serious," she said.

"Do I?"

"Yup. You look like you're seriously considering going nine rounds with Donovan on a king-size mattress."

Jodie smothered a laugh. "I'm pretty sure Donovan mentioned you were a preacher's daughter. Is that something a preacher's daughter should say?"

Callie let out a heartfelt sigh. "Everyone thinks we're either innocent virgins, or wild as sin. I'm somewhere in the middle of those extremes."

"Except on a king-size mattress with your husband," Jodie teased. "Then you're wild as sin."

"Of course." The other woman grinned. "Now, I hear you were supposed to be Cole's male-order bride, but I definitely get the feeling you'd rather snuggle up with Donovan."

"Oh, that was subtle."

"You're stalling, Jodie."

Jodie couldn't be offended. Callie Fitzpatrick had a merry smile and directness that was refreshing. And buried beneath her decidedly *un*subtle remarks, was a genuine concern for Donovan.

"It's complicated," Jodie murmured.

"It always is. Are you in love with him?"

Wow. Jodie looked at Callie and lifted her eyebrows. The woman didn't pull any punches. She went straight to the heart of the matter. It was just her luck to fall in with a bunch of die-hard romantics.

Jodie's gaze swept back to Donovan and she frowned. "I'd be a fool to fall in love with him," she said, yet her voice wasn't nearly as convinced as it should have been.

"He's a terrific guy. What makes you thinks it's foolish?"

Yeah, *what?*

The reasons *not* to fall in love were getting fuzzier by the minute. For all of Donovan's easygoing charm, he wasn't reckless. He was careful with the children, balancing caution with an understanding of their desire to explore the world. And even though he was an active sportsman, Jodie realized it wasn't because he was trying to prove something—to himself or the rest of the world. He just enjoyed life.

Wrapping her arms around her upper body, Jodie shivered. Life was unpredictable. There weren't any guarantees she wouldn't lose another husband, or that Tadd and Penny wouldn't lose another father. Donovan himself had pointed out the risks, no matter who she married.

"Jodie?" Callie's eyes were sympathetic.

"I'm not sure about love," Jodie said finally.

"But you're right about the snuggling part. Even if I'm not crazy enough to do something about it."

Callie grinned. "There's more than one way of going crazy. Maybe you should just get Donovan alone and let nature takes its course."

Chapter Ten

Callie's tongue-in-cheek advice about letting nature take its course stayed with Jodie throughout the next few days. Not that she planned on *taking* that advice, however tempting it might be.

But she couldn't help thinking about it.

In a way, the arrival of Donovan's friends relieved some of the pressure between them. With all the children and adults filling the house it was nearly impossible to be alone, though Evelyn did her best to push them together. Jodie was certain Donovan had told Evelyn and Shamus about her decision not to marry Cole, but they didn't say anything.

Jodie knew she should leave, if not for her sake, then for Tadd and Penny's. But she'd canceled her reservations at the motel, and Donovan had been right about the difficulty of getting a flight out of Alaska.

"You want to change your flight date in *July?*"

the travel agent had asked, incredulity in his voice. "It's the busiest time in Fairbanks."

"Yes, I know, but—"

"I suppose you could wait on standby."

Standby wasn't reassuring. Jodie had nightmare visions of camping at the airport for days, hoping three seats would miraculously open up on a flight.

In the end, she'd realized she would have to wait and hope it wouldn't be too hard on Tadd and Penny when they did leave. The agent promised he'd call if anything became available, though he'd remained pessimistic about the possibility.

On the last Saturday of the Golden Days celebration they attended the parade, then everyone piled into the cars for an event the children had been waiting with baited breath to see—the Rubber Ducky races on the Chena River.

Parking to see the beginning of the race was crowded and they ended some distance away. The four families joined a cheerful crowd of sightseers streaming toward the river, but Jodie felt oddly bereft. Penny was riding on Shamus's shoulders, and Tadd was busy with his new best buddy, Jamie Mc-Coy.

For the first time she had a sense of what it would be like as Tadd and Penny grew up, becoming independent and developing their own interests. Every parent experienced that separation, yet it was still hard to know that day was coming and there was nothing she could do but accept it.

A few feet away, Donovan looked at Jodie's solemn face and a pang went clear through his chest.

He'd welcomed the distraction of his friends, but it hadn't kept him from thinking about Jodie. Or from wanting her. Desire had become a permanent condition in his body, with little hope of relief.

Before he could think better of it, Donovan caught Jodie's hand in his own and laced their fingers together. "You aren't going to cry, are you?" he whispered. "I can take anything but crying."

"As Penny has discovered."

He chuckled. "So I'm a softie. Now, what's making you so sad?"

Jodie shrugged. "I was thinking about Tadd and Penny growing up. Parents don't get their children for long enough."

"Is that why you want another baby, to make it last longer?"

"I just want another baby. I guess—" she hesitated "—some of it is because I couldn't enjoy being pregnant with Penny. Mark was gone and I was so afraid I'd lose her." Jodie's voice shook.

Now Donovan was certain she would cry, and it scared the hell out of him, mostly because he'd do anything to make her stop. Jodie's tears wouldn't be a trick to get something she wanted; they'd be because she was hurting.

"It's okay. You didn't lose her. She's healthy and happy. I've never seen a happier child."

Jodie lifted her chin. "I know. I've told myself that a thousand times."

He gave her fingers a squeeze. "You're something, do you know that? You've had more reason than most women to give up, to just let someone else make all your decisions and handle things, but you don't."

"You thought that was why I wanted to marry

Cole," she reminded him. "So he could take care of us."

"Naw, that was another really dumb guy who looks a lot like me," Donovan said. "I, of course, am a perceptive, intelligent fellow who would never make such a foolish assumption."

"Of course."

"Are you laughing at me?"

Jodie had ducked her head, but not before he'd seen the laughter in her eyes. He didn't want to examine the satisfaction that went through him; anyone could have cheered her up, it didn't have to be him.

It's what a husband would do.

Donovan's lungs froze for a moment. He'd seen the give and take between his friends and their wives, the times they'd said just the right thing and made everything right. The moments of worry and stress made better by the touch of a hand or a kiss.

But it had never truly registered.

Marriage meant there was someone to share the joys and sorrows with. Someone to worry if you got home late. Someone who was a partner, as well as a lover.

Jodie was right—she had plenty to offer in a marriage. She'd be one hell of a wife for the right guy— soft and sweet and sassy, all at the same time. He just had to decide if he was the right guy.

It was a lot to comprehend all at once, and Donovan frowned thoughtfully. He'd been aware that his ideas about love and marriage were shifting since Jodie's arrival, and he'd fought it tooth and nail.

Now he wasn't so sure he wanted to fight anymore.

"Donovan?"

He hadn't realized he stopped walking until Jodie turned and tugged on his hand. "I'm coming," he mumbled.

Donovan looked ahead at the river. The rest of their party had already positioned themselves for the race. "I hope you're looking forward to this," he said. "It's one of the truly great sports. You ain't seen nothin' till you've seen rubber ducks race down a river."

"Are they a special breed, or just your garden variety rubber ducks?"

His eyes lit with laughter. "A special breed."

"Just for Alaska?"

Donovan touched Jodie's face, then stared at her mouth for a hungry moment. "Just for Alaska."

Jodie's heart began pounding so hard, she thought it would jump out of her chest. Kissing Donovan could become addictive. It was like eating chocolate—rich, melting across your tongue, sliding down your throat.

Donovan's finger touched the madly beating pulse point at the base of her throat and she swayed toward him. How much trouble could they get into, kissing with all these people around? They couldn't get too crazy, too out of control. It was safe.

"Hey, Mom, Donovan," Tadd shouted. "Hurry up. You're going to miss the race!"

Donovan smiled ruefully. "I like that kid, Jodie. But he's got a habit of interrupting at the most awkward times."

She wasn't sure if she was relieved, or exasperated herself by Tadd's ill-timed shout. There was something different about Donovan today. Since the afternoon his friends had arrived, he'd only spoken to her when the others were around, as well. Perversely it had annoyed her no end.

But today he was back to teasing her with the warm intimacy she found so disturbing...and appealing.

"Well, you know children," Jodie said huskily. "They have two volumes—loud and louder."

"Mooooom."

She lifted one eyebrow and grinned. "See what I mean?"

Donovan waved to Tadd, then gently swung their clasped hands. "We'd better go before he has a nervous breakdown."

When they returned to the house that evening the children were tired and happy having seen hundreds of rubber ducks "race" down the river. The light playfulness of the event *was* appealing, Jodie decided.

"Who am I kidding?" she breathed, shaking her head.

She'd had just as much fun as any of the under-eighteen crowd, but mostly because of Donovan. He'd jumped into the festivities with both feet and dragged her with him.

"I'm pooped," Ross McCoy declared as they piled into the house. "How about you?" he asked his wife, loving inquiry in his eyes.

"Fine, but guess who's hungry again?"

Ross stroked a strand of hair from Hannah's forehead. "I'll keep you company," he said softly. He took the baby and they headed for their bedroom.

Mary's feedings were a special time for the Mc-

Coys. It still gave Jodie a pang, but not because she begrudged the couple their happiness.

"I hope everyone is okay with cold cuts and stuff from the freezer," Evelyn said, plopping down on the living room couch. "How does potluck sound for dinner?"

"Fine." Jodie's mouth twitched, because Evelyn's idea of "potluck" was to pull things from the freezer, such as tamale pie, Irish stew and other prepared-ahead goodies. More than once she'd said it was potluck night, only to lay out a feast that left everyone stuffed and swearing they'd never eat again.

Jodie sank into one of the comfortable easy chairs. She was tired, but it was the kind of happy tired that went along with vacations and having fun.

The phone rang and Evelyn opened her eyes. "Donovan, can you get that?"

"Okay."

The second ring cut off in the middle and Evelyn smiled at Jodie. "We've gotten so involved in the Golden Days celebration, I haven't asked if there was something special you and the children wanted to do."

"We're having a great time," Jodie assured. "You don't have to worry about entertaining us."

"Not entertaining, just visiting. Besides, we're proud of Fairbanks. We like to show it off."

Jodie bit the inside of her lip. She ought to bring up the subject of Cole. Donovan must have discussed it with his mother, but she owed the other woman an explanation. Except it was hard to explain when she didn't understand herself.

"Jodie?"

She looked up and saw Donovan looking at her. His face looked carved in stone, without a trace of the carefree man she'd spent the day with. "Yes?"

"I need to talk to you. *Outside.*"

"Donovan," Evelyn protested. "What's wrong with you? Oh, dear…the phone, was it bad news?"

"No. It was just a travel agent. Coming, Jodie?" Donovan was having trouble hanging on to his temper, and he dragged a deep breath into his lungs.

Tell Mrs. Richards I've gotten her an earlier flight back to Florida. For tomorrow. Have her call to confirm the change in reservations.

Jodie obviously didn't understand what was wrong, and he resisted the temptation to yell or act like a caveman, even if it was exactly what he wanted to do.

Outside he swung around and glared. "Why didn't you tell me you were trying to get an earlier flight back to Florida?"

"I…" She cleared her throat. "Going home seemed like the best thing to do."

"You mean running away."

Her gaze narrowed. "That's unfair and you know it. I can't keep accepting your mother's hospitality when I've decided not to marry Cole. It isn't right."

"What about us?"

"There is no 'us.'"

"Like hell there isn't." Donovan grabbed Jodie's shoulders and gave her a small shake. "What if I said I was willing to think about marriage? Would you stay then?"

Jodie swallowed. "This isn't a game where I'm trying to win a husband. I'm not using marriage as a bargaining chip. And it isn't just me. I have to consider my children.''

"That's a rotten excuse. You know Tadd and Penny want me to be their father.''

"It's just that I can't—''

"Love me?''

She shivered and his hands gentled, stroking her arms.

"Isn't it worth finding out?'' he whispered.

Before he could saying anything else, Shamus strode across the porch, a worried expression on his face. "The park just called. Cole's climbing team—there's been an accident.''

Donovan froze and for an instant everything seemed to move in slow motion. *An accident.* His brother's climbing team. Images of the mountain rescues on which he'd worked rushed into his brain with horrific detail.

"What happened?'' He barely recognized his own voice.

"The details are sketchy. They don't think it's too serious, but several members of the team have been taken off the mountain and are being flown to Anchorage for medical treatment.''

"How is Evelyn?'' Jodie asked. She'd taken Donovan's hand and was holding it for all she was worth. If she'd ever doubted Donovan Masters's ability to love, it was erased by the pain and fear in his eyes.

"Worried, but she won't borrow trouble. She wants you and Donovan to fly to Anchorage immediately, and we'll look after the children.''

"But…'' Jodie looked between Donovan and his stepfather. She'd been convinced the Carneys knew of her decision about Cole; now she was being treated like a worried fiancée. "I shouldn't—that is, you and Evelyn should go with Donovan."

"Evie wants you to go." Shamus waited, then touched her cheek. "You have some sortin' out to do with both my sons, and they have to do the same with you."

Tears pricked in her eyes, both from concern and love for this kindly man, and the proud way he'd claimed Donovan and Cole as his family.

"Let's go, Jodie. I'll contact the Triple M office and tell them to get the plane ready." Donovan strode into the house, not even looking behind him. She didn't know if it was because he trusted her to follow, or because he didn't care whether she'd agreed to go or not.

"We'll call once we know anything," Jodie promised, giving Shamus a kiss.

She hurried to find Tadd and Penny, explaining she'd come back soon, and to mind what the Carneys told them. It was a relief to see them accept the news without a fuss—they'd come to love and trust the older couple as much as she did.

Jodie was worried for Cole in a friendly, distant way, but mostly she was worried about his family. Especially about Donovan. A sick feeling kept rolling in her stomach; if Cole was really hurt—or worse—then Donovan would feel guiltier than ever about the way things had worked out. He'd feel as if he'd betrayed his own brother.

In the bedroom Jodie packed enough clothing for a couple of days, her mind spinning with a dozen disjointed thoughts. Donovan had said he was willing to consider marriage, but he'd said nothing about being in love with her.

He didn't have time, her hopeful side argued.

It's usually the first thing a man says.

Right, and he thinks you were saying you couldn't love him.

"Quiet," she muttered crossly. There were more urgent things to worry about, such as Cole, and how badly he might be injured.

Donovan was already waiting by the Jeep when she ran down the porch steps. He helped her into the passenger seat, then jumped behind the wheel with a minimum of wasted motion. He was plainly on edge, but he kept his speed at the legal limit. At the airport they went in at a different gate than the one used by the passenger airlines, and in short order had climbed into the company's small private jet.

It was when the door closed that Jodie remembered this was the first time she'd been in such a small plane since Mark had died. She drew a quick breath and her heart gave a funny little skip before settling into an even pattern.

It was all right. She didn't have to worry, not with Donovan. She trusted him more than she'd ever trusted another man.

As though he'd read her mind, Donovan picked up her hand, kissed it, then put it back in her lap. "I'm a good pilot," he said. "I wouldn't fly if I thought it was unsafe."

"I know."

"Would you rather sit in the back?" He motioned to the cabin. "It's more comfortable than the copi-lot's seat."

The cabin was nicely appointed, even luxurious,

but Jodie shook her head. She'd rather sit next to Donovan and keep him company. "This is fine."

They taxied out to the runway and lifted off. If the circumstances had been different, Jodie might have enjoyed the view out the window, but there were too many things to think about.

"Mom packed some food," Donovan murmured after they'd reached a cruising altitude. "It's in the bag I put behind the seat."

"I'll get it." Jodie pulled out the soft-sided cooler and unwrapped a sandwich. Ham and Swiss cheese was piled generously on the bread, and she handed it to Donovan. "Can you manage that?"

"Fine." Donovan took a bite and chewed without really tasting the food. Coffee and cookies were consumed with equal detachment.

There were two critical events going on in his life—his brother's possible accident, and the fact he'd fallen in love with Jodie Richards. He couldn't do much about Cole until they got to Anchorage. And naturally he'd handled the second event with unparalleled clumsiness.

Okay, so he'd been furious to discover Jodie was trying to leave town without telling him what she was doing. But the thing that had sent him over the edge was hearing the travel agent call her *Mrs.* Richards.

An innocent, completely reasonable thing to say—she *was* Mrs. Richards. She wasn't divorced, she was a widow. And it was a reminder that Jodie didn't want to fall in love with another man because she'd lost her first husband.

He glanced at her solemn face and grimaced. It wasn't the best time to resolve anything, but they had a long flight ahead of them. And it was bad enough worrying about Cole, without worrying whether he'd screwed things up too much with Jodie. He may as well find out sooner, than later.

"Why didn't you tell me about the travel agent, Jodie? Why did I have to find out about it like that?"

She shrugged her shoulders. "He didn't think he could change the reservations, so there wasn't much point in saying anything. Besides, I didn't know how to explain."

"Why not try, 'I'm thinking about leaving'?" Donovan didn't want to lose his temper again. It wouldn't convince Jodie he was the kind of mature, responsible man she could trust as a husband.

"And of course you would have said, 'Sure, I'll help you pack.'"

"That wouldn't have been my first choice. How much warning would you have given us before heading to the airport? A day...an hour?"

"Donovan..." She made a helpless gesture. "It just seemed like we were tearing each other up."

"And you wanted to be safe again—no chance of getting your heart broken. Why didn't you stay in Florida in the first place? Why come five thousand miles to marry a man you've never met?"

Jodie pushed aside the sandwich she'd been trying to eat. Her stomach couldn't deal with food and Donovan's questions at the same time.

"I thought it was a compromise," she said. "After Mark's accident I closed down, just like my father did when my mom died. It was a safe shell where I couldn't be hurt. Then I decided I didn't want to live like that, so I thought I could have a comfortable mail-order marriage.''

Donovan didn't say anything for a long while, and she wondered if he was offended by what she'd said. It was honest. She'd never pretended to Cole that she expected to love him. Maybe that was why Cole had gone climbing—he'd decided he couldn't face marriage to a woman who wanted nothing more than companionship.

A chill crept over her skin and she shivered. If Cole was dead, or hurt, it could be her fault.

From the corner of his eye Donovan saw Jodie turn pale. He swore silently. It was thoughtless to bring her on this flight. Planes had to be a terrible reminder of what she'd lost. Reaching into a compartment, he pulled out the down parka he always carried.

"Wrap up in this," he said softly. He'd needed to deal with overwrought passengers before, and he didn't want it to happen with Jodie.

"I'm all right."

"Please, hon. You're nervous and it'll help warm you up."

"I'm not nervous." But she took the parka and cuddled into it, her green eyes dark with emotion. "Donovan, do you think Cole doesn't want to get married after all?" she asked, startling him.

"What makes you say that?"

"If he went on the climb because he changed his mind, then I'm responsible. Maybe it was me, not so much the idea of marriage. Because I didn't expect us to fall in love. Because I didn't *want* it."

Donovan's fingers tightened on the controls, and he took several deeps breaths. "Cole is responsible for his own actions. He would have gone on this climb regardless of what plans you'd made. As for changing his mind...I happen to know that's exactly what happened. But it wasn't because of you, he simply wasn't ready to get married.''

"You knew all along? Why didn't you tell me?" The color flooded back into her face with a flush of anger.

"I found out the night we went to his house. On his desk there were some drafts of a letter he'd tried to write. Do you really think I would have kissed you if I'd thought Cole was still in the picture?"

"Don't do me any favors."

"That isn't what I meant. Dammit, I want to marry you."

Jodie gulped and decided this wasn't something they should talk about. Not until they'd gotten to Anchorage.

"Let's talk about this later," she whispered.

Donovan cast her an incredulous glance. "Later? After what...I just said?"

"Now. Don't say anything more until we know about Cole."

"You think that could make a difference?"

"Yes, I do," Jodie snapped. "I know about men, and their honor and the idiotic notions they can get. And I'm not going to spend the rest of my life with a man who's feeling guilty and wondering if maybe, just *maybe,* he betrayed his brother."

"You're the one with idiotic notions."

Jodie crossed her arms, perfectly annoyed, but a moment later she sighed and a tear trickled down her cheek.

"I'm sorry," she whispered. "I know you're worried about Cole, and I've acted like a witch."

"Oh, God. Please don't cry."

"I'm not." She sniffed and straightened in the seat. "Let's just talk about something else. Anything but the last ten days."

"That's going to be difficult. The last ten days have been the most important in my life."

"Please, Donovan. You've got enough to think about without us ripping into each other. I mean, I'm sure Cole is all right, but you'll keep worrying until we get there."

"Okay."

Donovan thought hard—he'd give anything to erase the regret on Jodie's face. He knew she'd wanted to be reassuring and helpful, but the uncertainty between them, and the strain of flying had overwhelmed her...not to mention his own hard-headedness. When the time was right, he'd apologize.

They landed in Anchorage an hour later, and a car was waiting to take them to the hospital. Their driver said he'd heard the climbers had arrived, but still didn't know the extent of anyone's injuries.

As they walked into the emergency room, Jodie caught Donovan's hand and squeezed it. He looked at her, the somber expression in his eyes lifting for a moment.

They rounded the corner and the first thing Donovan saw was his brother, leaning on a pair of crutches and chatting up a red-haired nurse. Actually, heavy-duty *flirting* was a better description. His leg was encased in a white cast that ended just below his knee and he had a small bandage on his fore-head.

"Cole."

Cole tore his attention away from the buxom nurse and waved with one of his crutches. "Hey, bro. Hey, Jodie. You look just like your picture."

Donovan's concern dissolved into anger. He'd imagined his brother deathly injured or worse, and all Cole could say to him was "Hey, bro"?

"What happened?" he asked between clenched teeth.

Cole sniggered. "We all feel stupid, that's what. We'd gotten to the peak, and were coming down. I guess we got a little careless, and the next thing you know I've got a broken ankle and our team leader has a busted tailbone. Sitting down is going to be a real pain in the you-know-what." He winked at the nurse, who giggled obligingly.

"That's all you're going to say?" Donovan exploded. "What about Jodie? Is flirting and joking around more important than talking to your fiancée? Don't you realize what you've put us through?"

"It's okay, Donovan," Jodie murmured.

He felt her shaking and turned to apologize for Cole's behavior, only to see her laughing silently. Their eyes met and a laugh rose from his own chest, as well.

When Jodie could talk she looked at Cole again. He *did* resemble Donovan, but without Donovan's mature sensuality.

He looked like...a brother. Or to be more specific, a brother-*in-law*. And he was a little shame-faced, having trouble meeting her eyes.

"You're not ready to get married, are you?" she

asked. They needed to get it out in the open, before anything was said, before Cole discovered his brother had proposed to her. Though the sight of Cole hitting on a nurse had to be worth a thousand words. He obviously wasn't ready for marriage with her or anyone else.

Cole shook his head, relief flooding his face. "I'm really sorry. You came all this way for nothing."

Jodie just laughed again and gave him a hug. "Not for nothing," she whispered in his ear. "Instead of a mail-order bride, how does mail-order sister-in-law sound?"

"Really?" Cole drew back and looked between Jodie and his brother, a wicked grin growing on his face. "What *have* you been up to, bro?"

Donovan didn't take the time to wonder what Jodie had said to Cole. He could explain later about finding the letters, that he'd only kissed Jodie after learning of his brother's change of heart. Right now he needed to know if she was going to marry him.

Without giving Jodie a chance to protest, he grabbed her arm and dragged her down the hall. At the first empty room he pushed her inside and closed the door.

"Donovan?"

Well, maybe he needed to touch her first. With a low growl he snatched Jodie close and spun until her back was to the door and she couldn't leave, couldn't do anything but feel his body pressed full-length to hers. He had to believe she loved him, had to believe in the fairy tale. The alternative was too terrible to contemplate.

"You're marrying me," he said.

"I am?" Her green eyes laughed up at him, teasing, yet they also seemed to be waiting.

Donovan's grip gentled, but he didn't release her. He dropped a kiss on Jodie's forehead, then the tempting curve of her neck. He knew what she was waiting to hear and he searched for the words, knowing they would decide his future.

Finally, simply, he realized there were only three words that meant anything.

"I love you," he whispered. "I've been waiting for you my entire life and didn't even know it."

Tears spilled over in Jodie's eyes and Donovan kissed them away.

"I know you're afraid to love me, but I'm not going anywhere, except to follow you," he vowed. "You think you're stubborn? You haven't seen anything yet. If you go back to Florida you'll find me camped on your lawn. Your father will have to arrest me. You can hire—"

Jodie clapped her hand over Donovan's mouth. The tip of his tongue teased her palm, darting in and out between each of her fingers. When she could no longer take the sensual torture, she dropped her hand to his chest. His heartbeat was fast and hard, belying his calm exterior.

All things considered, she didn't have a choice—her heart had already made its own decision. "I love you, too," she breathed.

For an instant Donovan stared at her. "For sure?"

"Forever," Jodie promised.

"That isn't nearly long enough," he said. "But I guess it'll have to do."

Her sweet smile was the last thing he saw before taking her mouth in a deep, soul-satisfying kiss. Together they'd be everything a man and woman could be: lovers, best friends and a family.

Epilogue

"How does that feel?"

"Wonderful." Jodie looked down at her husband as he rubbed her foot, pressing his thumbs into the arch with gentle, circular motions. She moaned as he found a particularly vulnerable spot and her head dropped back on the pillow.

"You shouldn't have walked so much today," he muttered. "We don't have to do everything in one day—the Golden Days celebration lasts more than a week, so there's plenty of time. You're not in any condition to be so active."

"Nonsense." Jodie patted her round tummy. "The doctor says I'm disgustingly healthy. He doesn't suggest running a marathon, but normal exercise is fine. Besides, I love being up here with everyone. You're not going to make me sit everything out. Hear?"

"I hear."

Donovan kissed the curve of Jodie's foot and continued his massage. It didn't matter how many times the doctor said she was fine, he couldn't help worrying. But so far her pregnancy was progressing smoothly, with none of the problems she'd had while carrying Penny.

"You have experience with having babies," he murmured. "This is my first time."

"You're a major worrywart. I'm surprised the obstetrician hasn't started charging for all those frantic phone calls you keep making."

"They're perfectly legitimate concerns."

Jodie lifted her head again. "Sweetheart, you called him in the middle of the night because you thought the baby was kicking too much. Then an hour later you called because you thought it wasn't kicking enough. I'm surprised you didn't suggest he move in with us."

"I did. He reluctantly declined." Donovan grinned and concentrated on rubbing his wife's ankles.

They'd stolen a few minutes to be alone, but he knew it wouldn't last. Easing his hands up Jodie's legs, he cupped the tight mound of her stomach and kissed it.

"Hello, little one," he whispered.

Tears glistened in Jodie's eyes. Donovan had embraced fatherhood with a great enthusiasm, and marriage with an even greater passion. Tadd and Penny had accepted him without question, avoiding some of the normal adjustments between new stepfathers and children. Sometimes she thought it wasn't possible to be happier.

"You still don't want to know if it's a girl or boy, right?" she asked.

"Nope. I like surprises."

They'd had the usual sonograms but they'd agreed they wanted to do things the traditional way. When the baby was born they would know if they had a new son or daughter; in the meantime they just wanted to know it was healthy.

Her husband stroked her breasts with a touch that was less soothing, more arousing. She quivered, responding instantly to the caresses she'd come to know so well.

"I don't think we…oh…"

Donovan pulled the extra pillows from beneath Jodie's shoulders and lay beside her, scattering kisses across her throat and neck. The more he made love to his wife, the more he needed her. And she was so beautiful, glowing with that special happiness of carrying his child in her body.

She could have one, or a dozen more babies, whatever she wanted. He'd give her the world if it was possible.

"What do you want?" he breathed against her fragrant skin. "Diamonds? Emeralds? How about a Ferrari?"

"How about you?"

He smiled and untied the shoulder ribbons of her maternity sundress. "You *have* me."

Jodie smiled with blinding satisfaction. "That's all I want."

Donovan tugged the fabric away, freeing her breasts. They were rounder with pregnancy, her nipples darkened to a reddish brown. And so sensitive. He could see them tightening in anticipation, with just the way he looked at her.

That was one of things he adored about Jodie. She

was so generous in her loving, so responsive...so honest. Everything she did was honest. When they had a fight she got angry fast and cooled off even quicker. Everything was out in front, with nothing held back.

Gently he brushed the darkly crowned centers of her breasts with the back of his hand and she moaned.

"This isn't fair, Donovan. There's a whole houseful of people out there. We can't make love an hour before dinner."

"Yes, we can." With the tip of his tongue he traced the gold nugget nestled at her throat. It was part of the necklace-and-earring set he and Tadd had given her for Christmas.

"Donovan...no. The kids will bang on the door and open it up, wanting permission for cookies and ice cream to ruin their appetite. My father is going to suggest we move to Anchorage so he can see his grandchildren more often. Then your mother will want to know if potluck is okay for supper, and whether I think green is a good color for the quilt she's making for the baby."

"I *locked* the door," Donovan whispered, sweeping her dress onto the floor. He peeled off his shirt and shoved his jeans down his legs. "Someone else can tell Tadd and Penny 'no.' Cole will distract your father. And Mom wouldn't come near that door—she knows perfectly well what we're doing."

"Oh." Jodie shivered with delight. It seemed deliciously risqué to make love in the crowded house, with everyone from her mother-in-law and own father stomping through the hallways.

"Besides, if Mike and Callie can get away with it, then we can."

Laughing, Jodie slapped Donovan's chest. "You weren't supposed to notice them slipping out the other night."

"We have to make love," he said softly. "It's the anniversary of our second kiss."

"I see. Well...maybe if we're fast."

With a low, hungry growl Donovan slid over her. "Honey, the way I'm feeling, fast is the *only* way it'll happen."

The desire already humming in Jodie's veins turned into a brushfire. At six months pregnant she wasn't as supple as usual, but it seemed to satisfy her husband. His fingers were everywhere, and his mouth, teasing and tempting and finally tipping her over the edge.

A long time later she floated back into herself, becoming gradually aware of the sounds outside their bedroom. Donovan was holding her spoon-fashion against his chest, his hand once more stroking the taut curve of her belly.

"I think we'll have to rejoin the land of the living," she murmured. "And I hate to admit this, but I'm hungry."

"Good. You're too small. I'm sure the doctor is wrong about the correct height and weight stuff. Are you sure he said you weigh enough?"

Jodie chuckled. "I've gained every ounce I need to. If I ate the amount you think I should, I'd be the size of a moose."

"I just want everything to be all right."

"I know." She kissed his shoulder, then slid out of the bed. "We better get dressed."

When the obvious evidence of their lovemaking had been erased, Jodie and Donovan headed for the living room, though she was certain she still had an indecent smile on her face.

"It's awfully quiet," she said.

"I think everyone's outside playing softball," Donovan murmured.

"Not everyone," Jodie's father said from his chair by the window. He folded the newspaper he'd been reading and watched his daughter and son-in-law with calm approval.

General McBride had decided on an early retirement and was now living in Anchorage. Jodie had worried he wouldn't be able to handle the change, but he'd become active in the historical society and was working on a special military museum. He'd also made friends with Shamus, frequently visiting Fairbanks in the past months.

Donovan's own relationship with Shamus had grown to the point he often called his stepfather "Dad" and phoned routinely just to chat.

"I'll go help with dinner," Jodie said, giving Donovan another kiss. She left the two men together, knowing they'd find things to talk about. Donovan had a gift with her father, blending just the right amount of self-assurance and respect to please the retired general.

"Hello, dear. Did you have a pleasant...nap?" Evelyn asked, looking up from the salad she was preparing. "You've got a lovely glow on your cheeks."

"Mom, you're incorrigible," Jodie scolded. But she wasn't bothered. Evelyn didn't have a mean bone in her body.

"I know. That's what Shamus tells me."

Jodie went to the large freezer and began poking in its contents. She had a craving for spinach lasagna, and she'd seen some in there earlier. Mouth watering, she pulled two large containers from the freezer. "Do you think this is enough for dinner?" she asked.

"We'd better thaw a third one, but you shouldn't be doing that," Evelyn scolded.

"I'm not a guest anymore, I'm family."

"Yes, you are," Evelyn said contentedly. "I'm so glad *one* of my sons had the good sense to marry you."

"That's not fair, Mom," Cole protested as he walked in. He winked at Jodie and snagged a cookie from a plate on the counter. "Donovan saw her first. I never had a chance."

Jodie just smiled and shook her head. Cole loved to tease Donovan about "stealing" his mail-order bride, but he still wasn't ready for marriage, preferring to taste family life vicariously through his brother.

The baby gave a strong kick and Jodie laid her hand on the spot. She loved being pregnant and hoped they would have at least one more after this one was born. Both Hannah and Callie had confided they were trying again, too, so in another year Evelyn could have a whole new set of babies to love and spoil.

"Cole's just jealous," Donovan said as he strolled into the kitchen. He slid his arms around Jodie and she smiled, leaning against him. She knew there would be bad times along with the good, but every minute together was precious.

"Happy, Mrs. Masters?" he whispered.

"Delirious," she said. "How about you?"

"In heaven." And he kissed her, just to prove it.

* * * * *

**Intimate Moments is celebrating
Silhouette's 20th Anniversary with
groundbreaking new promotions and star authors:**

Look for these original novels from
New York Times bestselling authors:

In August 2000:
A Game of Chance by **Linda Howard**, #1021

In September 2000:
Night Shield by **Nora Roberts**,
part of NIGHT TALES

Don't miss
A YEAR OF LOVING DANGEROUSLY,
a twelve-book continuity series featuring SPEAR—a
covert intelligence agency. For its equally enigmatic
operatives, love was never part of the mission profile....
Sharon Sala launches the promotion in July 2000
with *Mission: Irresistible*, #1016.

In September 2000, look for the return
of **36 HOURS**, with original stories from
**Susan Mallery, Margaret Watson,
Doreen Roberts** and **Marilyn Pappano.**

And look for:
Who Do You Love?
October 2000, #1033
You won't want to miss this two-in-one collection
featuring **Maggie Shayne** and **Marilyn Pappano!**

Available at your favorite retail outlet.

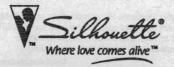

Silhouette®
Where love comes alive™

If you enjoyed what you just read,
then we've got an offer you can't resist!

Take 2 bestselling
love stories FREE!
Plus get a FREE surprise gift!

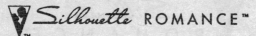 **Silhouette** ROMANCE™

He's experienced and sophisticated.
He's mature, complex...and a little jaded.
But most of all, he's every woman's dream.

He's

AN OLDER MAN

Don't miss this exciting new promotion from
Silhouette Romance and your favorite authors!

In June 2000 look for
PROFESSOR AND THE NANNY
by Phyllis Halldorson, Silhouette Romance #1452
Nanny Brittany Baldwin was the answer to single dad
Ethan Thorpe's prayers. But that was before the lovely
young caretaker started showing up in his dreams....

In July 2000 Stella Bagwell brings you
FALLING FOR GRACE
Silhouette Romance #1456
One glance at his alluring new neighbor had
Jack Barrett coming back for more. But the cynical
lawyer knew Grace Holliday was too young and
innocent—even if she was pregnant....

Only from

 **Silhouette**®

Where love comes alive™

Available at your favorite retail outlet.

COMING NEXT MONTH

#1462 THOSE MATCHMAKING BABIES—Marie Ferrarella
Storkville, USA

With the opening of her new day-care center, Hannah Brady was swamped. Then twin babies appeared at the back door! Luckily Dr. Jackson Caldwell was *very* willing to help. In fact, Hannah soon wondered if his interest wasn't more than neighborly....

#1463 CHERISH THE BOSS—Judy Christenberry
The Circle K Sisters

Abby Kennedy was not what Logan Crawford had expected in his new boss. The Circle K's feisty owner was young, intelligent...and beautiful. And though Abby knew a lot about ranching, Logan was hoping *he* could teach *her* a few things—about love!

#1464 FIRST TIME, FOREVER—Cara Colter
Virgin Brides

She was caring for her orphaned nephew. He had a farm to run and a toddler to raise. So Kathleen Miles and Evan Atkins decided on a practical, mutually beneficial union...until the handsome groom decided to claim his virgin bride....

#1465 THE PRINCE'S BRIDE-TO-BE—Valerie Parv
The Carramer Crown

As a favor to her twin sister, Caroline Temple agreed to pose as handsome Prince Michel de Marigny's betrothed. But soon she wanted to be the prince's real-life bride. Yet if he knew the truth, would Michel accept *Caroline* as his wife?

#1466 IN WANT OF A WIFE—Arlene James

Millionaire Channing Hawkins didn't want romance, but he needed a mommy for his daughter. Lovely Jolie Winters was a perfect maternal fit, but Channing soon realized he'd gotten more than he'd wished for...and that love might be part of the package....

#1467 HIS, HERS...OURS?—Natalie Patrick

Her boss was getting married, and perfectionist Shelley Harriman wanted everything flawless. But Wayne Perry, her boss's friend, had entirely different ideas. Could these two get through planning the wedding...and admit there might be another in *their* future?

CMN0700